WITHDRAWN

# THE GIFT HORSE

# THE GIFT HORSE

MARY McMULLEN

PUBLISHED FOR THE CRIME CLUB BY
DOUBLEDAY & COMPANY, INC.
GARDEN CITY, NEW YORK
1985

All of the characters in this book
are fictitious, and any resemblance
to actual persons, living or dead,
is purely coincidental.

LIBRARY OF CONGRESS CATALOGING IN PUBLICATION DATA

McMullen, Mary, 1920–
The gift horse.
I. Title.
PS3563.A31898G5    1985      813'.54      84-13763
ISBN 0-385-19872-8

Copyright © 1985 by Doubleday & Company, Inc.
All Rights Reserved
Printed in the United States of America
First Edition

*To Alton*

# THE GIFT HORSE

# 1

Waking in the night, hot and restless, Darrell Hyde thought, Really, it would be no trick at all to kill Aunt Lally.

He had been lying on his back. He turned and raised himself on one elbow and gave his head a hard shake.

Had the thought been part of a dream, so real, so eerily sensible, that it had waked him up? Or had he, in full command of his wits, formulated it?

Or seen an imaginary flash in the darkness, lighting things up for a second or so, and translated it into words?

And had he spoken the words aloud? He listened for any faint echo of his own voice in the stillness of the room.

There had just been the rustle of the sheet as he moved a leg experimentally to make sure that he wasn't still asleep. That was the only personal noise. And no, he wasn't asleep.

Three floors below the window of this grim little room on Fordham Road in the Bronx, trucks lumbered by, and from a block or so away a man shouted something in Spanish. Darrell had here and there picked up a little Spanish. The man was shouting that he was going to kill somebody. The sound of a bottle smashing interrupted this announcement at—Darrell glanced at the illuminated dial of the electric clock on the bedside table—four o'clock in the morning.

Was that the voice which had entered his own dreaming, or his half waking?

Maybe the flung or wielded bottle had already done its work, done the killing in the night.

He fumbled for the switch of the lamp on the table, found

it, and looked around the room to try to get some kind of bearings.

Nothing familiar about his surroundings to anchor himself to, or test himself against. The room had been lent to him the day before. He was making his way down by buses from Rockport, Massachusetts, where he had picked up a few weeks' work painting boats, shining brass, scrubbing decks and galleys in preparation for the Rockport sailing summer.

On the last leg of the journey, his seatmate, a battered-looking man of forty or so with a guitar case on the rack over his head, fell into conversation with him. Was he new to the big town? What was he heading into, what kind of job, or was he just looking around?

Darrell said that, no, New York wasn't new to him, and he hadn't a job right now. When they got out at a rest stop and had a quick beer, the man said, "If you're down to rattling pennies, look, you can have my room for three or four days. It's in a lousy dump in the Bronx but there's a bed and a toilet —private. I'm going on through to Newark for a week or so. The room's paid for till the end of the month. Here's my key. Drop it in my mailbox when you leave."

In one of his sudden flashes of rage Darrell thought, Do I strike everybody—even this nobody—as being some kind of hopeless joe? But he smoothed his face, smiled, said, "Thanks a lot," and accepted the key and the little piece of paper with the address scribbled on it.

A room, okay, all taken care of, but he still needed some getting-along cash.

"Oh no, darling, not again," groaned Darrell's sister Jennifer when he came, trying to sound offhand, to his request. Her words were without meaning; no warmth to the "darling," and as far as "not again," surely she knew he'd always come to her first, before approaching either of his brothers. He always had, for—how long?—nine, ten years.

He had walked from the Port Authority bus terminal to her apartment on East Sixty-ninth Street, walked into another world. On his way, crossing town from west to east and striding through rising block numbers, he noted with interest that not only the buildings and streets but the people in them underwent a marked change. West, a lot of overweight people, short people, very thin people, blacks and all kinds of skin colors. Then, gradually, the people on the sidewalks in the Manhattan twilight got slimmer, straighter-backed, taller, better dressed. More incisive in motion, eyes brighter, skins clearer. West, only a few dogs; east, breed after handsome breed being taken for an evening stroll.

He had chosen to walk up Park Avenue because he liked the great sense of openness and space of this broadest of New York boulevards. Turning east again on Sixty-ninth, he looked with disfavor on a pair of superb silver-white Russian borzois being walked by a doorman. But the other Darrell said to himself, Oh God, what beauties. He had once worked at a kennel in Westchester and remembered that "borzoi" in Russian meant "the swift one."

He hadn't called Jennifer from the bus terminal because he thought it was very likely she would say she was just on her way out the door—if, that is, she was home at all. If their circumstances were switched, he might very well offer the same excuse. And there was only one chance in ten she would be at home, not out amusing herself somewhere, or dashing, on the job, to Paris or Cairo or Mexico. She was a writer of television commercials, a fifty-thousand-dollar-a-year v.p. at a top New York agency, a name, a somebody, very much of a somebody. Look at Jennifer, he had been told by various family members a hundred times. Only two years older than you.

Darrell stood in the disconcerting mirror-walled twenty-by-thirty-foot living room and looked at Jennifer. Or at six or seven Jennifers, reflected and re-reflected. Tall, for a woman, about two inches under his five feet ten. Thick shoulder-length fling of mahogany-brown hair, long elegant face, the mouth not right now at its most charming. Riveting green eyes. Geranium-red velveteen pants, a white silk shirt, a cummerbund-belt affair of crushy black leather wrapping her narrow waist. Black ballet-practice slippers from Capezio. The successful young executive, At Home.

Before he found a cool easy answer to her rhetorical "not again," she went on, "I thought—I don't know who told me —that you'd be in Rockport for the summer. It sounded nice." Her tone said, Why *aren't* you in Rockport for the summer, instead of here begging in my living room?

This attitude on her part was new. She'd been up to now good-egg Jennifer, the least given to scolding of any of them, the check resignedly signed, or cash if she had plenty of it around. Had she been crossed in love? Or had someone turned down one of her television scripts?

He felt tired and soiled after the long three-stage bus trip. He glanced down at the chair nearest him, which looked as if it had been freshly reupholstered five minutes ago, a deeply tufted tub chair in the palest apricot silk.

"Okay, sit down—of course," Jennifer said, following his glance. "I think that nice chair near the window." That nice chair was covered in sleek fawn-colored glove leather and wouldn't show dirt. Although he had started out with his jeans washed, and they looked all right to him.

"I squeezed three weeks out of Rockport," he explained. "But after that there wasn't—so many of these boat people like to do their own work—and after a while it gets you in the back—" Hand at the small of his back, illustrating.

Wasn't she going to offer him anything to drink? Should he shame her into it by asking for a glass of water?

Reading him, Jennifer said, "There's not a thing in the place except Perrier water. I'm on this marvelous fruit-and-Perrier diet, one quarter of a pound of lean meat at one meal a day."

"It's too bad it hasn't done more for your . . . usually nice nature," Darrell said, flushing pink, feeling whipped. "Surely you don't offer your man—or your men—Perrier water?" As far as he knew, there had been a man, one man after another, in residence at Jennifer's apartment. Love affairs or, all right, just plain affairs, sampled and then moved on from.

Perhaps due to the excellence of her diet, Jennifer produced a far richer blush than his. Rage, he thought. His first guess about this new nastiness of hers must have been right.

"There isn't a man on the premises at the moment," she said, and then blinked, smiled slowly, and let the words hang on the air.

As though she had somehow shocked herself too, after a moment she said in a changed, softer tone, "Oh, to hell with it. Just for now anyway. The cleaning woman keeps a bottle of scotch in her broom closet, as I know well and can't do anything about because you can't get any kind of help at all these days, much less competent help—Oh, sorry, darling, foot in the mouth again. I'll go and rob her for a change."

When she left the room, Darrell, restless, got up and prowled about. He stopped at a large, half-open box from Bergdorf Goodman tilted against a sofa arm, lifted the lid, saw something metallic blue and coarsely knitted with red yarn loops hanging out every few inches, the price tag in a fold of tissue paper. "1,890.00" said the price tag. He hastily replaced the box lid.

No longer able to bear any more of himself in the mirrors, he was standing looking out of one of the long windows in the south wall when Jennifer came back with a tray.

She poured her own drink first, two generous inches, added ice cubes and an ounce or so of water, then, "Help yourself." He fixed his drink, went back to his dirt-resistant chair, and lifted his glass. "Cheers to something, I don't know quite what. To, maybe, prying a J and B out of virtuous Jen."

The faint bravado of the words, the, he supposed, deliberate use of the shortened name of childhood, made him feel a little ill.

She took a long savoring swallow of her drink and became brisk. "Let's see, where are we? I'd ask you to dinner but I have to go out and play elsewhere. I suppose you have someplace to stay while you're in town?"

"Yes, a friend's apartment."

Her telephone rang and was answered seven times during the course of the next half hour, so that between these interruptions and those provided by his own mind, when he just closed his ears and went away, he could never exactly reconstruct the interview.

To begin with, she made out a check for two hundred and fifty dollars and gave it to him. "I know it's not much, but I'm flat stony, in the throes of buying a little cottage on Fire Island."

"Thanks, Jennifer." Flat stony, with a garment of some kind costing close to two thousand dollars in the Bergdorf box on the sofa.

"And anyway"—after a trip back from the phone, the call taken in her bedroom behind a closed door—"I'm breaking a solemn family promise, or just did when I wrote that check." She poured herself another drink. Her color was high. "Why should I be stuck with doing this?" she asked indignantly of her face across the room in the mirror. "But we did agree that whoever you came to first . . ."

"What promise? Agreed to what?"

Two more phone calls. Then he was told the story, or what, over a deep tremble of apprehension inside, he could retain of it.

Their father, Anthony Hyde, who had been transferred last year to the top echelon of the Cortlandt Bank's Bonn offices, had had to fly back to New York three weeks ago on business. They had had a family celebration in New Canaan, because one of the three days was Roger's birthday.

As though putting off something she didn't want to get to yet, if at all, Jennifer enlarged on the party. "A hundred and seventy-five people, and Martha had a steel-drum band flown up from Barbados, and Daddy met an old girlfriend and had a high old time . . ."

Tony had been in New York too, coincidentally, casting for his new film, and came along to New Canaan for the spree. "So it was a family reunion, almost—except for you. Of course, your birthday is a week after Roger's and we toasted you in absentia. Your thirtieth birthday. What a milestone. I'll never forget mine even though I'd like to."

The family agreement, and mutual promise, was as follows: The door was to be slammed on any more money to Darrell. It was bad for him, hopelessly bad. Now at thirty, he had to have a new outlook, a fresh viewpoint, and plan to make it on his own. It would be so much better for him that way. They had, for all these years, been crippling him unintentionally, trimming his sails, pulling rugs from under his feet by helping him when he should be helping himself.

"Of course you have talents—look at the rest of us. A vein of gold somewhere inside you. You just haven't started up your engine yet. I mean, darling, painting hulls, apple picking in Binghamton, playing chauffeur to a blind old rich man, that awful fizzle in the training course at the Bank, and back, and back, and back, all those flash-in-the-pan jobs, and before that dropping out of Yale and—"

She paused for breath. She didn't look directly at him, but at his face in the mirror. Darrell had managed to keep his features in order but his skin was pink and glistening with sweat. And his chest heaved a little; he was finding it hard to get his breath.

She took his glass from his hand and poured him another drink. "Of course it's hard being the baby of the family, but you're thirty now, rich ripe thirty. I don't think I said happy birthday."

"Your check—the Hyde Memorial check—says it." Calm if slightly breathless voice. He wanted to throw his drink in her face. But he needed it. And she might tear up the check, and he needed that too, or where—?

Church bells chimed the hour nearby and Jennifer looked at her watch. "Oh God, where does the time go? I must . . ."

There should be some way to get out of this, get out of here, gracefully and casually, but none presented itself to Darrell. He stood up and drained his drink.

"Thanks, anyway—" he began.

"What do you mean, anyway?" Jennifer sounded angry again and he wondered fleetingly if it was at herself or him or both. Her mouth had a doleful droop.

"I mean, thanks—I've got to be—and I should by now know my way to the door . . ."

Her head came up sharply. Did she think he intended that as a dirty crack of some kind? He hadn't; he had just not wanted to put her out any further.

She got up and came over to him. "Darrell dear, do begin by straightening your back. That slouch isn't exactly . . . But I know this hasn't been terribly nice for you, even though only the best is meant by everybody."

She hesitated and then, standing in the living-room doorway as he reached for the hall doorknob, "Here I go breaking promises again. But—"

He turned his head to her.

"Aunt Lally, now. I haven't seen the dear old duck in years and I don't know how she's fixed. But seeing that you're such a favorite of hers—perhaps if you bump into another emergency she might help?"

# 2

The American Airlines eleven o'clock flight to Albuquerque, now ten minutes from its scheduled departure, was fairly crowded. Darrell had by blind luck been assigned a seat by a window and there were only double seats on the window side, as against the six-in-a-row lined up massively in the center. The other seat was still empty.

It was two days after his interview with Jennifer. Yesterday, taking one thing at a time, as he told himself (never mind for the moment his family's thundering birthday-present heave-ho), he had made some telephone calls.

He had few close friends but a large loose circle of acquaintance which formed a species of unofficial employment agency. Hi, boy, how've you been? Things are tough here too. Jobs are tight.

He turned up two uninviting possibilities. Waiter, nighttime, at what sounded like a third-rate joint in Atlantic City, the Dash and Dot. Carrying drinks and food to terrible people brought in by the busload to lose their money and, what the hell, have a fling. Gambling had never tempted him, not that kind.

The other was short-term, on-and-off work in Brooklyn. "Man's renovating a house and doesn't want to mess with unions," his friend in Brooklyn Heights said. "There's a ratty old cellar he wants to turn into a family room. I have to warn you that the last fellow broke a leg falling through the cellar stairs—termites. You'd have to hack through a temporary way-in, in back, but before that you'd have to clear the . . ."

"Thanks," Darrell said hastily. "I'll call you later, there are a couple of other things that . . ." He didn't even bother to finish the sentence.

It hadn't been, following that call, a matter of sitting down calmly, looking things in the face, summing things up, making long-range definite plans. He had simply, at four-thirty yesterday, called three airlines and finally got a seat on American. Who says I'm a man without a country? he had asked himself with a twisted inward smile. There's always a place named New Mexico.

He had cashed Jennifer's check first thing yesterday morning, with the idea that she might have confessed her sin to one of their brothers and been ordered to stop the check immediately. Or had changed her mind all by herself.

"Crippling him unintentionally. Trimming his sails." He was at the teller's window of the Fordham Road branch of the Cortlandt Bank at seven seconds after nine o'clock.

The air fare to Albuquerque was $299 plus tax. He had eighty dollars of his own money but after breakfast and the bus trip to Kennedy he had less than ten dollars in his pocket. Aunt Lally, he thought, had damned well better be home. He had considered calling her to tell her he was coming to see her, but some instinct had warned against it. She might say that next month would be more convenient, or that (the Brooklyn job coming to mind) she had broken an ankle or hip or something and wasn't up to visitors.

But as far as he knew she wasn't a gallivanter, a taker of journeys. Unless she had changed a great deal. People, though, didn't take on new ways of life at the age of seventy-three, did they?

His seatmate arrived, a tall man with a heavily handsome face, looking to be in his thirties. Darrell, in fear of being trapped in conversation, opened his paperback but the man hardly glanced at him before putting away his fancy beige suede suitcase in the compartment above. Out of the corner of his eye Darrell gave him a swift, Hyde appraisal. Gray suit expensive, and looking too obviously so. Shining black Italian loafers with monogrammed gold buckles. Black and white striped shirt and an unfortunate white ribbed silk tie with a gold crown-shaped tiepin set with what might be little rubies. A strong whiff of sandalwood cologne. He opened a black leather steel-framed attaché case and, using it as a lap desk, began studying pieces of paper, a gold pencil in his right hand at the ready.

After takeoff, which always made him a bit nervous, Darrell, while keeping his gaze steadily fastened to the pages of Barbara Tuchman's *The Proud Tower*, went back to Aunt Lally.

He supposed he must have seen her before that time, but his first clear strong recollection of her was when, at the age of ten, he was taken to her by his mother and left with her for the summer.

He had had bronchitis and then pneumonia and it was felt that a summer in the hot, dry mile-high air would do him a world of good. The other three Hyde children were radiantly healthy, as were their parents.

He had once overheard his mother saying to his father, "But where did the poor lamb get it? His second-rate constitution?"

"Probably from Tom," said Anthony Hyde, with the very faint edge of contempt on his voice whenever he spoke of his brother.

Thomas Hyde, ten years older than Anthony, was married to Aunt Lally. They lived in what seemed to the young Darrell a modest sort of cottage, built of adobe, under cottonwood trees on a winding road called Andalusia Trail, in the northwest section of Albuquerque.

For a short time he felt the sensations natural to his age and circumstance: lonely, cruelly abandoned, tossed almost across the country to be gotten rid of just because he had been sick.

But soon it turned into a happy summer. Tom kind and quiet, always remaining in Darrell's mind as something of a background figure. Lally in her open easy way took to him immediately and gave him a warm, non-smothering, steady affection.

They had no children of their own. At least ten times during the summer, Lally would say, "Don't you think he looks like you, Tom? I do, I swear I do."

Life was serene at the little adobe house. Tom, who was a certified public accountant, came home gray and tired from his day's work downtown and retired to his pipe and newspaper when he didn't have to work nights in his office-den off the kitchen.

There were no near-neighboring children to play with, which was a relief Darrell didn't then identify: there was no one to have to compete with. He rode, timidly, a small elderly roan mare borrowed from a friend of his aunt's, up and down Andalusia Trail. He helped in the garden, weeding and watering the flowers and the vegetables. He read whatever he pleased from well-stocked bookshelves. He was allowed to sleep as late as he liked and found himself dazedly sleepy around nine or earlier every night. He turned the glorious kind of brown he had always envied in his two older brothers in summer.

And he was in ways the center of the house, the focus. A very odd feeling. A deep-inside delightful feeling.

When his father came out to bring him home, late in August, Lally said, "Well, to paraphrase the old saw, Anthony, you haven't lost a son. But we've gained one."

"Finally, thank God!" said the man in the seat beside him. Darrell looked up to see the lunch and drinks cart lumbering slowly toward them. Could he afford to spend money on a beer or so? He felt superstitiously that if he did spend the money, taking his aunt's presence at home for granted, the more likely she was to be there.

"Two scotch on the rocks for me," the man said. "D'you have Chivas Regal? Or Haig?"

"A can of beer, any brand will do," Darrell said crisply. And after this brief attempt at aggressive self-assertion, he retreated a bit. "Or—well—now that I think of it, it will probably be a while before you're back—make it two beers."

While drinking his Chivas Regal and eating his lunch, the man read through a sheaf of typed papers headed, "Users' Attitudes Toward Breath Deodorants, Based on a Sample of 1500 Nationwide." Darrell went back to *The Proud Tower*, noticed that he was still on the same page as at takeoff, and turned to the next page.

Lally asked his parents by letter if Darrell could spend the following summer there. "No," said his father to his mother. "I don't want this to turn into a habit. Tom's not all that good for him—poor gray Tom. And Darrell's all too prone to drift into the same nobody-and-nothing ways." This decision was reported promptly and accurately to Darrell by Jennifer, who had been nearby when it was made.

But the next year Lally simply sent his round-trip air fare. "You've probably planned his summer," she wrote, "but surely he can fit in a couple of weeks with us."

After that visit, the same arrangement was carried out every other year. Sometimes Darrell went eagerly. And sometimes unwillingly, when he began to feel a sense of debt, the burden of some kind of demand on him.

He spent his own money, made working during the summer at a hamburger stand in Burlington, Vermont, to go out to Albuquerque the September when his uncle died. It had been a quiet neat death, leukemia. His parents couldn't or didn't make it to the funeral because they were at a banking conference in Geneva.

When he was preparing to go back East, Lally said, "I know young men don't like to be tied down, but how would you like to stay here and live with me? There are good jobs around and you have a taste for the open air." Darrell, who was then twenty-three, said no as politely and kindly as possible. By now, back home, no one expected very much of him. He knew Lally would expect a lot of him.

As he expected little of himself, the prospect was unfaceable.

He went back once more when he was twenty-seven. They had exchanged occasional letters betweentimes, always in hers the tactfully put "Do tell me what you're up to now." Without actually lying, he gave his rapidly changing activities a glossy surface. "It's not everybody's way, but it's mine, trying, say, five or six things to find out what you really want to spend the rest of your life doing. Some of my friends have terrific jobs and totally miserable existences."

Although he had often been tempted to, he had never asked her for money.

Early in a bad raw March when he had day-to-day, street-slogging work for a consumer research company in Chapel Hill, North Carolina, he got a letter forwarded to him from his parents' East Eighty-first Street duplex. He hadn't lived there for years, but as his own mailing address changed so often, he used this one for convenience; besides, it looked impressive when he filled out job applications.

Lally wrote that she hadn't been feeling her best all winter and that seeing him would buck her up a great deal, as soon as he could find a free week or so. Air fare enclosed.

He went reluctantly, with a vision of serving tea and toast to a once hale and now frail woman propped up on her pillows in bed. He was surprised to find her looking remarkably well, up and around, with her ruddy year-round sun and wind color in good glow.

"I took a turn for the better when I got your call saying you were coming," she said, and something twitched at her left eyelid which he could swear was a wink. But he had never seen a wink from Lally. He used her first name now. "Let's drop all this aunt nonsense," she said. "We're friends. Very old friends. Since you turned ten."

The day before he was to leave she cooked him a good send-off dinner. Roast chicken, mashed potatoes with her marvelous delicate gravy, Waldorf salad, a fresh-baked cinnamon-scented apple pie with cheddar cheese. After dinner, she poured coffee and two generous brandies.

She leaned back in her chair at the kitchen table and said, "Now that we're fed and comfortable, I think it's only fair to tell you that I finally faced up to it and made a will, in February. You're my sole heir, Darrell. I don't want any thanks and to-do and I intend to live forever but you know, now."

He blinked at her and took a gulp of brandy. All he felt at the moment was acute embarrassment. And a remote hot prickle of . . . what was it, unworthiness?

In an apparent switch of a troubling subject, she said, "It was very hard on Tom, too. Anthony was always—at school, at work, in his social life, in his marriage, always wrapped around with his own blaze of glory. It wouldn't have been so difficult if he was the older brother, someone to look up to and emulate. But he was—is—ten years the younger. That isn't to say you mustn't find your own feet. I know you will."

Lying in bed that night, Darrell thought, She means I take after Tom. Not only in appearance but in general capability.

Tom, who was a nothing right straight through to the end of his life.

That's what she's willing to me, too.

## 3

After lunch, Darrell finished his second can of beer, eyes on his book, aware of his seatmate's snapping shut the attaché case, yawning, turning his head slightly toward him. He had developed considerable skill at reading attitudes, even reading minds. Perhaps, he had decided, it was a defensive art that some people didn't need at all.

The man was probably, in view of his jeans and shabby sneakers, wondering if he'd be worth speaking to, even to alleviate boredom and pass the time.

Decision made. "Where are you heading?" the man asked. "Chicago or Albuquerque?"

"Albuquerque." Gaze still on page twenty-seven.

"Live there?"

"No. East."

"Where, East?"

"Manhattan, when I'm at home."

"That's my base too. I'm with"—white grin of pride—"Horter Industries."

"I've never heard of them," Darrell said, closing his book but keeping his finger in the fold.

"Well, maybe in your field—whatever it is—you wouldn't have." A touch of irritation, condescension in the voice.

"My father," Darrell said, "is senior vice president and second man to the top in the Cortlandt Bank."

"Really?" Eyebrows up, strong examination of his face and untidily clipped hair and plaid shirt open at the throat. Behind the one word were some more: Who do you think you're kidding?

Darrell felt heat under his skin and hoped it didn't show pink on his face.

"My brother Roger is with Helvetius. Maybe you've heard of *them?* Wall Street brokerage house. He's doing very well there. He makes a hundred and fifty thousand dollars a year. Lives in New Canaan, big fieldstone house with stables."

The other now allowed his mouth corners to lift in open amusement. "Tell me more about this wonderful family of yours. In Manhattan."

"Well, Tony, my other brother, is mainly based on the Coast. He's a writer-director of films. You may have heard of him. Tony Hyde. He figured the sci-fi vein would finally be mined out and took a walk backward to the fourteenth and fifteenth centuries. Plenty of blood there, battles, castles, sex, torture if you go for that kind of thing. I guess you're old enough to have seen *The Lady and the Dragon* without parental guidance. So far it's grossed forty million. It's his fourth picture."

"Yeah," the man said. "I'm old enough to have seen and heard a lot of real crazy funny things."

"Then there's my sister Jennifer." Darrell found he couldn't stop himself. "She's a vice president of an advertising agency, does television commercials, and—"

"And how much does she make a year?"

"Fifty thousand. But with traveling pretty well all over the world thrown in for free."

"That's nice. What"—grinning again—"about your mother? Is she a famous international hostess or something?"

His cheeks were really hot now. How could the honest-to-God truth make you blush? "I suppose in ways, yes. At the time of her marriage she was a well-known interior designer. She still takes on an occasional job for the fun of it. Last year, a ten-room condominium in Trump Tower."

"Well, let's get back to number one, always the main thing, right? What do *you* do?"

The natural, the obvious question, but it caught Darrell unprepared.

He hesitated.

"What's the matter? *Your* vein mined out?"

A memory came to his aid, a car trip taken with his uncle when he was fourteen, up to the top of the Sandia Mountains.

"No, not mined out. Just wondering how to put it in layman's terms. I'm a forestry man, always liked the open air. The Cíbola National Forest wants an analysis of growth patterns on various slopes, and then there's an erosion problem to be gone into, and an Asian sap disease that has to be brought under control . . ."

"And how much does that net you, your analysis and so on?"

"I'm too modest to tell you."

"Modest? You?" The man unbuckled his seat belt and got up. "Speaking of forestry, nature calls."

Encountering an attractive flight attendant on his way back, he murmured, "That guy next to me, see him? Plaid shirt. What's he on, do you think?"

Tactful and pleasant, "Nothing as far as I know. Would you like to change your seat?"

"No, but if you could hunt me up a magazine, a *Time* or *Newsweek* or something, then I could look buried in it."

He need have feared no further disclosures from Darrell, who in the few moments by himself sat bewildered, staring at nothing, wondering what had gotten into him.

But thank God the Sandia Mountains had come to mind. He could hardly tell the man that he was going to Albuquerque to look a gift horse in the mouth.

He opened his book again, determined not to utter another word until they landed.

Looking a gift horse in the mouth. He liked putting it that way. It sounded sensible, practical, and committed him to nothing.

After all, he had never thought seriously about the property, about the will at all. It had seemed a speck on a remote horizon.

But it would certainly be, yes, only common sense to see what things were worth in today's dollar values: the house, the land. Come to think of it, he had no idea of the size of the property. With the small gardeny front yard, the walled flower gardens in back, the vegetable gardens beyond, and hadn't Lally said the field stretching back to woodland, where the horse borrowed for him had grazed, was theirs, too?

They had bought it at least thirty years ago, long before the words Sun Belt appeared in the language, and before immense portions of the population began to move out of the cold and rain and snow into the heat and light. Whatever they had paid for their house and land—probably slowly and patiently coping with the mortgage—would now at least have doubled itself. Or tripled or quadrupled itself.

Lally had written four years ago that she had had a happy mortgage-burning party with a few friends from down the road. Now it was all free and clear.

Did she have any valuable pieces of furniture? He mentally roved the rooms of the adobe house but he was by no means a trained assessor of household·objects. Even though he had grown up among French and English antiques here, Eames and van der Rohe and Saarinen there, and the rattans and wickers and old painted cupboards and tables of houses by the sea in summers. There was a heavy, rich, carved look to some of Lally's things. Spanish, or Indian? Carefully collected —or casually acquired? Books in the public library ought to provide clues.

The place might need work, things seen to, perhaps fences wanting repair, a roof that leaked. Talking as he had of his superbly functioning family, it seemed to him—this survey of his inheritance, no matter how distant its prospect—to be a matter of simple, basic efficiency.

There were other aspects which should be looked into, or intelligently guessed at.

How much, actually, was Lally worth? She got no doubt some form of Social Security and possibly a widow's portion of a pension of Tom's, but that income would cease when . . . she did. Did she have holdings of any kind, stocks, bonds, savings, money market accounts? Perhaps another piece of land bought as an investment? Of course he couldn't ask her outright but there were other, subtler ways to information.

What was the actual state of her health? Since her bad winter three years ago, she hadn't in her letters complained of anything except her annoying postnasal drip and in the springtime, when the winds blew so violently, her dust allergy that sent her into bouts of sneezing.

He didn't even know if she came of a long-lived family. Her maiden name was Grover and he had an impression that her family had lived in Nyack, on the Hudson. No brothers, he was sure of that. One sister, who had died some time back. So you couldn't measure by that. And of course her parents would be long since dead or there would have been some mention of them over the years. But might there be, suggesting an extended life span in the Grover blood, a nonagenarian Grover uncle or aunt still hanging on in Nyack?

Another thing. While he had never thought her temperamental, was there a chance that, put out by the long gap since his last visit, she would have changed her mind about her heir? Found a new favorite? Someone who went out of his or her way to be nice to Lally, bring her library books, lend her records, help out in the gardens?

Some people used their wills as a form of amusement, a

mirror of moods, a sharp and swift revenge if their anger was aroused.

That girl Lydia, now. She'd be about his age or a little younger. He had met her on his last visit, Lally telling him a bit of her history beforehand. "Her mother walked away from them when she was nineteen or so—after *twenty* years of marriage—and finally married a man—very rich, I believe— younger than she is. They live in Switzerland. It would be nice if you took an interest in Lydia, dear. In her own way she's quite attractive."

But there had been a lot of people, it was Lally's birthday party, and all he could remember of Lydia was very short dark hair and large lavender eyes. At that time he had been involved with a girl of his own. She remained his own on and off until she took a good sharp look at the future, said a fond goodbye and good luck to him, and married a biochemist with Du Pont who was making a handsome salary and had even handsomer prospects.

Was she still alone, still unmarried, Lydia? Had Lally remained close to her, interested in her, sorry for her, stuck as she was with an ailing father who Lally had said was understandably embittered?

A feeling at first chilled and then hot came over him.

He should have thought of this project long ago.

The plane started its descent from 37,000 feet approaching O'Hare Airport. The man beside him got up and reached down his suede suitcase. He addressed Darrell for the first time in twenty-five minutes. "Want your duffel bag while I'm up?" Darrell saw him smiling at the sight of the stained and shabby bag, once tan with once uncracked red leather straps and handles.

"No, thanks. It'll be a while."

He was subjected to the man's unblinking and what could be called fascinated stare at his ear, his cheek, his hair, his sneakers, for at least ten minutes. "Well, now I've seen everything," the man said. "Or, rather, heard everything. Chicago's my stop. Nice town."

"Well, good luck with Morton Industries," Darrell said.

"Not Morton. Horter. And good luck with saving Cíbola National Forest, whatever and wherever that is, for posterity."

A final flick of a verbal whip. You nobody, you, trying to con a man who knows his way around, in Manhattan, in Chicago—you name it.

Darrell felt himself hot-faced again. Why had he let himself in for this?

But, seeking explanations, he thought that maybe what had happened was an exorcism of sorts. Leaving the Hydes, the shining Hydes, behind him, on this plane.

He had a feeling that one way or another he would not be heading back toward them, any of them, for a long while.

If ever.

# 4

"Well, here we are. Hey, good luck. Nice to have met you."

The girl stopped her dusty Volkswagen in front of the house on Andalusia Trail. Darrell, emerging onto the sidewalk at the Albuquerque airport, had only waited for several minutes before a likely-looking car drove up. A plain, fat middle-aged woman got out and said through the window, "Bye, dear, see you in a week, be good," and carrying a small suitcase, went past him through the automatic doorway.

Darrell moved to the half-open window and looked at the girl at the wheel. "On your way into town by any chance?"

She leaned across and gave him a careful looking-over. "Sure. Want a lift?" She was plain, too, with friendly freckles and long brown hair.

"If it isn't any trouble. Andalusia Trail much out of your way?"

"A little, but that's okay."

"I could pay for the extra gas . . ."

"Forget it. Hop in."

On the way, she asked him if he was a native or what, and with the idea that now was the time to start being careful and sensible, he said he was visiting a relative but that he thought he might look for work, things back East were slow. (He was also rehearsing for Lally.)

"Not so hot out here either," she said. "I mean, hot as hell" —with a grin—"but along job lines, that is."

She drove fast and efficiently and in twenty-five minutes they had reached Lally's house. He thought about asking for

her name and telephone number as a courtesy but then she'd
want his in exchange. Better not. He thanked her and got out
of the car.

With the two legs of the flight and the two-hour layover in
Chicago, it had been a six-hour journey but now by Mountain
Time it was only about three-thirty. The house, set fifteen
yards back from the street beyond a low adobe wall, proclaimed Lally's presence, or someone's presence. He could see
the cool broad dark hall through the screen door and the
living-room windows to the right of it were open.

For perhaps the first time, he took a thorough look at the
house. Adobe in good shape, no cracking or flaking, all its
corners gently rounded. Not a big house from the front, but a
long one, with an ell at the rear. Old crooked juniper tree to
shade the living room, immense cottonwoods on both sides.
Driveway to his left, grass-grown in the center, going back to
the neat white-painted garage. The garage doors were open
and he saw her elderly car, the same blue Pontiac, inside.

Twenty years ago his uncle had paved the front area in
slate, large unevenly shaped pieces skillfully fitted together,
with mosses and small flowers growing now through the
joins. Close to the low outer wall there was a great clump of
yellow and mahogany-colored iris. The place had, it occurred
to him, its own quiet charm.

He hesitated a moment before approaching the screen
door. Should he have called her, after all, and not taken her
totally by surprise? Suppose her heart wasn't what it might
be.

And there was the possibility that her greeting would be a
forbidding or distressed one, because she'd been informed by
the family of their decision about him and been asked to co-
operate. But in that case, would Jennifer have slipped her
name to him as a sort of, let's face it, last resort?

Knocking firmly, he called through the screen, "Surprise,
surprise! Guess who!"

After a few seconds of silence, there was an answering cry from the depths of the house. Lally rushed into the hall and gazed unbelievingly through the screen, then flung the door open.

"Well, I will be damned," she said, and gave him a quick hug.

Darrell surveyed her anxiously to see if there was any sinister meaning underneath this welcome. Lally seldom swore.

She was a large, strong woman with dust-colored hair worn short and uncurled around her broad ruddy face. Her blue gaze was direct and forthright, as it always had been. She had never bothered herself with feminine wiles and ways, wore no makeup, and dressed carelessly, not concerned with what went with what. Today, blue chambray pants, a white cotton shirt with the sleeves rolled up, leather sandals on feet which gave visible evidence of traipsing about in garden soil.

"I suppose you're just passing through?" she asked. "Otherwise it would be too good to be true. Come into the kitchen and we'll have ourselves a whiskey. I feel a little . . ." She put her hand to her heart and smiled. Darrell was horrified to see a sparkle of what might be tears in her eyes.

He set his bag down in the hall and followed her through the dining room into the kitchen. The house looked as it always had, a little untidy, a little dusty, pleasantly comfortable if a little shabby.

The kitchen was large and shadowed now in the afternoon, looking east to the Sandia Mountains. Lally, not given to idle chatter to fill spaces of silence, got a bottle and glasses out of a wall cabinet and poured generously.

"Help yourself to ice and water if you want it. I'll have mine as it is, considering."

They seated themselves at the square red-painted kitchen table. Lally took a swallow of her whiskey and then said, "Now, young Darrell, speak."

He stumbled a little here and there. Things slow back East. Only one job to be had, architectural renovation in a house where a man had been killed by a fall—the whole place coming apart with termites. And somehow, the feeling of a turning point on his thirtieth birthday. "New places and faces," he inserted a little desperately. "You know what I mean . . ."

Christ, was he sounding like a drifter? Which of course was what he had become; the first time he had let the word say itself in his mind.

She saw the naked anxiety in his eyes. Over an inward flinching on his behalf, she came quickly to his aid and finished his speech for him.

"Well, I call that sensible. The South, the Southwest, the West—they're the places to be from here on in. Everybody else is what you could call emigrating. I think it's high time you did too. While you're young and strong and—I suppose —free?"

"No serious entanglements," Darrell said with a relieved grin. "I lost my one and only to a biochemist a couple of years back and I'm not in any hurry to get burned again."

"You'll stay with me, I hope? At least for the time being, until you find your work. We'll put our heads together over that. See what we can come up with."

"I'd like to stay for a bit, yes—if I won't be putting you out."

"You know better. I suggest you take a few days off—well, today's Thursday anyway—before you start job hunting. You look a little pinched. And thin. You can help me in the garden and pick up some sun."

"It rained every other day on my last job, in Rockport," Darrell said. "I can sure use some." He finished his drink and got up. "Mind if I stroll about and look around to see if anything needs mending or fixing?" With an attempt at restoring as much confidence as he was ever able to feel, "You have no idea of all the things I'm good at."

"Do. And as we're going to live nice and comfortably together for a while, I'll stick to my own routine and take a nap, I usually do around this time."

Kind and welcoming as she had been, he found it liberating to be alone, not having to listen to the tone of his own voice or worry about the expression on his face.

And free to take a long, leisurely survey of what was now not only his present, but his future.

He opened the kitchen door and went out into 100-degree sunlight. There were three walled gardens behind the house, one of which he had just entered. The walls were eight feet high and six inches thick, adobe painted a soft honey color. The gardens were of uneven sizes, an oblong, a square, and a circle. They had been built, Lally had told him, by the original owners of the house to protect their plants and flowers from the tremendous winds that blew from late February until May or June.

Their fresh healthy green grass was surrounded by two-foot-high troughs of earth at the bases of the walls. Darrell, having once spent a summer as an under-gardener in Lenox, Massachusetts, knew some of the flowers, the vines, and the shrubs, but couldn't identify them all. Each garden had a door to the next, usually left open. The door of the round garden, giving on to the big open space devoted to vegetables, had an oval mirror set top to bottom into it, lending to the scene an air of surprise and romance.

Hands in his pockets, he gazed at the mirror, hardly noticing his reflection. I never realized how nice these gardens are, he thought. They ought to add a great deal of value to the place. How many houses in this town have segmented walled gardens?

As he recollected, most people here hated it when the winds blew. Enough to drive you crazy, they said.

The vegetable garden was large but not unmanageably so, and well cared for. Did Lally do it all herself? Was she capable of hour after hour of work in the formidable heat of the sun or did she have paid help? Find out.

He strolled between rows of tomatoes, corn, potatoes, zucchini, radishes, onions, lettuce, and something that might be Jerusalem artichoke but he wasn't sure.

The fact that she now had a regular afternoon nap didn't indicate a thing. Ever since he could remember, his mother had had a nap between four and five, getting up for a leisurely bath, changing into something long and pretty, and serving or being served drinks before dinner. His father was there sometimes, or when he was late or away from New York, attractive chattering friends.

Beyond the vegetable garden, an open field stretched away, two old apple trees bending toward each other in the middle of it. The far end of the field was unfenced but marked by a long grove of pines, called by some piñons here. Where *did* the property end? And how large was this field? Certainly a good deal more than half an acre.

A very nice piece of open land, with the Sandias rising purple against the cloudless blue afternoon sky. A very desirable place, he thought, for someone to build a house.

But what about zoning? Could another house be built here, even though it would be a good distance from Lally's? Investigate. Just as a matter of interest.

Zoning, though, at least in this part of Albuquerque, must be a little odd if not downright careless. To the left of her property was a rather grand house set almost invisibly far back from the road at the end of a double row of cottonwoods edging the drive. To the right, not sixty yards from Lally's, was a tumbledown establishment, close to the road, with a pile of worn rubber tires on its old sagging porch, another tire hanging from a tree for a child's swing, a crookedly leaning garage, the whole acquiring a certain rowdy gaiety from immense old trumpet vines which had grown over one of the broken windows as well as up and around the chimney.

His investigations, his speculations—or perhaps it was the whiskey?—suddenly made him feel a little dizzy. Puzzled and disoriented. He sat down on a tree stump to regain himself and found it a comfort to remember not only that he had traveled a long way and a long time, but that he was now five thousand feet above sea level. Probably as you got older you felt the change more, for a few hours or a day or so.

Older? Thirty. Thirty was in a way young.

He looked at the sky and the mountains, and then glanced down at a monarch butterfly flickering over clover heads. A strange feeling began under his rib cage, and a new one, a faint glow, a mysterious calm.

The thinned air again? No. For the first time in his life, it seemed to him he had a graspable future.

But just as well to file it away: don't look too closely at it right now.

## 5

At ten o'clock, seeing Darrell stifling a yawn, Lally said, "This is my usual bedtime and for tonight I think it's yours too. But first, follow me around. You'll often be up later than I and you can take over this little task."

Going from room to room, he watched her lock-latch every window, lock and bolt the front door, the kitchen door, the door from Tom's office-den into the garage, after the garage doors themselves had been locked. This was new to him. The only door he remembered being locked at night—sometimes —was the front one.

Lally explained during the process. "There's been trouble not far from here. A bunch of young toughs throwing bricks, breaking plate-glass windows at the shopping center on Fourth Street. Only one house broken into as far as I know, half a mile down the trail, the usual stuff stolen . . . television, motorcycle, I forget the rest. So I bought some hardware to make a tight ship for myself."

His room, the guest room, was at the far end of the ell. "You'll want your window open, but let's see . . . yes, the screen is still latched. I'll just look and see if there are any spiders in your sink." She opened the door to the small lavatory and turned on the light. "No spiders."

Feeling uncomfortable, and finding his breathing restricted for some reason, Darrell said, "It's the same everywhere. Not just in big cities. When I was in Rockport an eighty-thousand-dollar cruiser was stolen. Out of a locked boathouse."

"Don't tell me horror stories at this hour. You're probably

too bushed to read in bed tonight—tomorrow I'll give you a
hundred-watt bulb instead of this stingy sixty." She folded
back the flowered cotton comforter and white top sheet and
gave the pillow a plumping pat.

Darrell was in bed and deeply asleep within twenty minutes. Lally, who ordinarily drifted peacefully off soon after
retiring, lay awake, gnawed with worry, an entirely new kind
of worry.

Darrell's face. The tilted sloe-dark eyes, their lightlessness
kindled now and then with anxiety. The black eyebrows
down-slanting from the center, as if questioning, or asking
for sympathy, something that had never struck her before.
The black hair, loose and silky as a child's, spilling in a
crooked homemade haircut and really too long for this day
and age, out of style. The dejected carriage of head and shoulders when he thought himself unobserved. The fumbling for
words, which didn't go at all with the deep rich resonant
Hyde voice.

"New places, new faces, you know what I mean . . ." At
thirty, not knowing yet what he wanted to do or where he
wanted to be.

Had it been a terrible mistake, telling Darrell that he was
to be her heir?

Had it somehow robbed him of drive, or will, or direction?

Knowing that sooner or later there would be a house he
could live in, a ground of his own to stand on. Or sell.

He hadn't been blessed with the financially usable talents
or abilities of Roger, Tony, Jennifer, or his parents. If he had
his own special gift it had yet to manifest itself.

He had once told her that as a child he had loved working
with modeling clay. Before he entered Yale, he asked his father if he could go to art school instead; if not, could he enroll
specifically in the Yale School of Art? His father said no.

"Your great-uncle was an artist, and a rip-roaring queer into the bargain." Subject dropped for good and all.

A thought as chilly as a northeast wind struck her. Would Tom have drudged away at a job he hated if he thought there was something promising around some not faraway corner? Perhaps yes. Perhaps no.

Was it too late to do anything about it?

Administer some kind of spinal medicine? Turn a cold shower on warm if distant hopes?

Or at least insert a question mark.

Think about it. Think very hard about it.

Darrell woke at seven to a new sort of feeling, a freshness and stirring of undefined hopes.

He found Lally, who had always been an early riser, sitting at the kitchen table drinking her hot black coffee, which she liked generously sugared. Her eyes looked shadowed and tired but her voice was brisk.

"Eggs and bacon as soon as I have my transfusion. Help yourself to a cup."

Darrell was not much of a talker when just out of bed and normally neither was she. But, frying bacon, she said, "Let's do a little exploring. You said something about being offered work in architectural renovation. That's quite a big field nowadays. There's your cousin Adam, now. I'm told he's doing awfully well, has the firm pretty well to himself now that his father's semi-retired. He's just finished a whole *village* of condominiums on one of the better Hawaiian islands, the name escapes me. I'm sure he'd be glad to use you if you're good at your work. Of course, it would mean going to San Francisco, where he's based . . ."

Go off to San Francisco? Did she really, then, not want him here? Why?

Adam Satterlee was a cousin on his mother's side, and very much one of Them. At thirty-nine, an internationally known

architect, and married into the bargain to San Francisco
sugar money.

(Darrell had often thought that it would be such a joy if
there was another down-and-outer somewhere in the family.
Just one other would be enough.)

Hastily, and truthfully, he said, "I'm not actually trained or
qualified—I just do what they tell me to do. Plastering walls,
or taking the plaster off the bricks beneath, or—"

"Oh. I'd thought"—she lifted out three strips of crisp
browned bacon, laid them on paper toweling, and put three
more strips in the pan—"that perhaps you'd taken night
courses, or something. You mean, just, journeyman labor?"

He blushed. She wasn't sounding like herself. He wished
he didn't have to sit here, trapped, listening to her.

"Well, never say die. I had another idea. You have such a
good voice, really a beautiful voice—have you ever tried to
market it? Say, disc jockey or some such thing at a radio station. Or doing commercials, radio commercials. I know they
have advertising agencies out here and most of the local talent
is awful. You might begin calling around today and making
auditioning appointments with the various radio stations and
agencies and so on."

He couldn't offer her another immediate backing away, although he thought her suggestion laughable. You would have
to have experience, connections, pull; or at least a powerful
show-biz brashness. "It's a thought, I might try . . . even
though I've never been any prize at the performing arts. I
suppose, as a spin-off, telephone solicitations—'Won't somebody buy my violets?' "

Lally poured excess grease into an empty coffee can and
broke four eggs into her pan. "I wouldn't wish that kind of
work on you or anybody else. A man called me yesterday to
try and sell me a cemetery plot." She laughed. "I told him he
was barking up the wrong customer, and I had plans to be

cremated, and in any case not until twenty-five years from now. I forget—your eggs over or not?"

"Sunny side up, thank you."

"No," Lally resumed. "What you want is a good line of work you're good at, with a decent income and a solid future. Thirty's all right, thirty's fine, but you wouldn't want to be still casting about, here and there, say at the age of forty?"

"God, no." Christ, no, *no.*

She put his plate in front of him and sat down with hers. "Lots of opportunities here." Determined cheer in her voice. "Between us we'll swing it."

He couldn't wait to get away from her. He ate his breakfast quickly, apologizing for that. "Tastes so good . . . and the air here makes you hungry, not to say greedy . . ."

In a few minutes, moving at a saunter, he fled the kitchen.

Waking briefly at dawn, he had had a memory come back to him and went now to verify it. Lally's brother Bill had stayed with her and Tom decades ago, for a year, when he was taking some graduate course or other at the University of New Mexico. Hadn't he had quarters somewhere in the garage?

The garage was two-storied and eaved. It angled off the ell, facing the road. It was comfortably out of sight of the kitchen windows. Lally must go around unlocking when she got up; the green-painted doors were ajar. He went in past the blue Pontiac and saw the wooden stairway at the rear. On one visit, he had asked where the stairs went and Lally said, oh, just to a place where Bill had bunked when he stayed with them, and that ever since it had been a storeroom.

The door at the top of the steps was not locked. He opened it on a massive and dusty collection of old trunks, metal filing cases, cardboard cartons. The windows were dirty and cobwebbed. It might be wise to be careful where he put a hand, and to remember that his ankles were bare: one of the fea-

tures of New Mexico, which called itself the Land of En-
chantment, was black widow spiders.

Swift investigation—having here and there to shove aside a
filing cabinet or a stack of boxes—showed him that the second floor had been arranged as a compact apartment. There
was the center room where most of the stuff was stored,
which would be a living room. On one side, under the slant of
the eaves, there was a narrow bedroom with a folding bed
and a chest of drawers in it. On the other, a small but efficiently workable kitchen, and beyond the door at one end of
it a bathroom. No tub, but a stall shower cased in opaque
ribbed plastic.

Plans began to simmer enthusiastically in his head. Clear
out the junk. Furnish it with secondhand stuff or rent it un-
furnished. The views from the windows at the end of the
main room and the bedroom were, even through the blur of
dust, pretty.

Maybe put window boxes full of flowers outside, they always dressed a place up. Maybe install folding inside shutters
to control the light, for a touch of class. Maybe cover one
living-room wall in mirror squares, to give an illusion of
doubled space.

Even if he never again lifted a finger, the rent would bring
him in—how much? Take a look at the ads for apartments for
rent in the local paper.

Funny that Lally hadn't thought of doing this long ago.
Maybe it was because the one-story main house didn't have
an attic and she had no place else to store this useless-looking
stuff. But you'd think, if she needed the money . . .

Maybe she didn't need the money.

How much money did she have?

You couldn't always tell from the way people lived. For
instance, his mother had a friend named Cora Jennings who
lived in an immense naked loft in SoHo, wore her hair in a
braid down her back, and spent a good deal of her time sitting

on a Navajo rug weaving straw baskets. You never would dream, his mother had said, that Cora was worth three million dollars.

Lally might have, in the bank, in a savings or money market account, a few thousand. Or fifty thousand. Or more.

There were too many things he didn't know about and couldn't even make an educated guess about.

And this was just plain unbusinesslike.

## 6

Darrell, running down the wooden stairs at the rear of the garage, decided to say nothing at the moment about the apartment project. It might sound pushy, and like an attempt to make the place a more profitable operation, which in turn could raise a doubt or furrow a brow.

Finding Lally washing the breakfast dishes, he said, "What can I do in the garden for you this morning?"

"The round garden's a mess—I suppose you still know a weed from a flower?"

"Yes. A while back I took an extension course in botany." An extension course as an under-gardener; but it was a little prop to pride.

"And the potatoes need . . ." She turned from the sink. "But first, you might make a couple of phone calls. To radio stations. Dip a toe in."

The telephone was in the living room, and he remembered that there was another in Tom's office-den, but she could hear him, in his timid uncertainty, from there; it would look funny if he closed the door.

He looked in the yellow pages of the directory on the lower shelf of the little carved wood table where the telephone stood. He called, at random, KHFM and KUNM. The first said politely that it was fully staffed, in response to his statement that he was interested in work as an announcer. He felt a fool, but this was just an exercise to be gotten through. The second informed him that this was Public Radio, as well as the station of the University of New Mexico, and was staffed

by its own students, except for the d.j.'s, who were all volunteers. A kind girl at the other end of the line added, "Unless
. . . are you a recognized authority in some field? Southwestern art, or Indian affairs, or pueblos, or something?"

"No," Darrell said. "Thanks. I'm just a voice."

She said, "You might give me your name and phone number. Who knows?"

Well, Lally had said a couple of calls. Last he'd heard a couple was two. He went into the hall, out the front door, and around the house to the walled gardens. Report the negative results to her later, when he would be glistening with the sweat of honest toil.

He remembered that the garden tools were kept in a half-partitioned room in the garage, alongside the space which was large enough to hold two cars. This sectioning-off was used for the two big galvanized-metal garbage cans, an old workbench of Tom's with his tools still hanging on the pegboard behind it, and shelves at the far end holding clay pots and tools, muddied gloves, trowels, dandelion picks, the usual paraphernalia of gardening.

He picked up a useful hand tool, wooden-handled with a sharp metal blade side for hacking and powerful claws on the other for cultivating and for yanking stubborn stuff out of the soil.

Rakes, shovels, spades, hoes, and a spading fork leaned in a corner beside the shelves. He thought he might need the hoe for the potatoes, picked it up and hefted it, and then saw another one behind it, new, with a heavy triangular metal head that came to a sharp point.

Into his head came unbidden a drift of words, Lally's voice last night, "There's been trouble not far from here. A bunch of young toughs . . ." But of course the garage was locked up at night.

There were people around who did pretty awful things in broad daylight.

He spent an hour in the round garden. It was unshaded, which was one of the reasons why everything grew so magnificently. Lots of the plants had already been there when they moved in, Lally had told him. A third of the honey-colored wall was covered with a powerful old bush of deep pink roses, which he could identify as damask and not tea rose from the heavy, winy, spicy smell which in the heat was a little intoxicating.

He went on hands and knees around the circular raised trough, relentlessly removing even the smallest intruder, using the claw so that the earth, what little showed of it, was a rich tended brown crumble, receptive of air and watering. He went back and got the manual lawn mower and mowed the round grass plot to perfection, finding only one dandelion, which required a third trip to the garage for the dandelion pick.

Then, dripping by this time, he attacked the potato rows with the triangle-headed hoe. He stopped in the middle to take a red bandanna out of his pocket and tie it in a band around his forehead because the sweat running into his eyes was blinding him.

He had almost finished the first of two rows when Lally appeared. She laughed at the sight of his headband. "From the neck up, you look ready to play tennis at Wimbledon," she said. "A far cry from my day—those lovely white clothes and visors. Come sit in the kitchen and have some iced tea. Or beer if you'd like. You've been out in this sun for an hour and three quarters and I don't want heat prostration on my hands."

Darrell thirstily agreed to iced tea, with fresh mint bruised in sugar to give it an edge. Now that the sun was high, the kitchen was in welcome green shadow.

In a way that sounded casual if not absentminded, Lally said, "Mail's just come. I hope you left this as your forwarding address? Anyway"—she took a sip of her iced tea—"a letter from my niece Joan, in Carmel, in California. My poor sister Wendy's daughter. You probably don't remember Joan, I think you met her once when you were eleven or so."

Darrell placed Wendy as dead for some years, and did have a vague memory of a little blond girl with brown eyes.

"Sad, really. Had an awful time with her husband, but in the end he divorced her, not she him, and she has two little children on her hands. She's having a terrible time making ends meet. I worry about her a great deal. She's finally landed a job, far beneath her level, clerking in some kind of variety store, but she writes that business is off and it may not last . . ."

Darrell, who was not interested in other people's sad stories, listened politely. Lally's eyes on his face became fixed. In what seemed an unconnected way, she went on, "Before I did the dishes I went out to the car to get a bottle of detergent I forgot to bring in. I heard footsteps overhead, and for a moment I was a bit scared, but then I thought, that's Darrell, saying hello to every corner of the place again. It was, wasn't it?"

"Yes." He raised his glass with a steady hand and drank. "I can't remember ever having been up there before, so I went exploring. You have an interesting collection of spiders but I didn't spot any black widows."

"Well, soon I'll get to my point. Joan's health's been bad, cold after cold, then bronchitis—shades of you when you first came out here!—and I have a feeling that she'll be needing help, real help. Naturally I worry about the children, no father, no future, at least right now. One's five, one's seven. Boys. It occurred to me, hearing you overhead, that there are perfectly good living quarters up there."

"All I saw was boxes and files and things . . ."

"Oh, there's a kitchen, bath, nice little bedroom too, the boys could sleep on a sofa-bed affair in the living room. Now, I don't intend to lay out a lot of money but between us I think

we might clean it out and do a little painting. And"—smiling
—"get rid of my spider collection. Just so she'll know she's
not to be left helpless, and that there's a haven somewhere in
this naughty world."

"Good idea," Darrell said, finishing the rest of his iced tea.

*I think it's only fair to tell you you're my heir.*

*She'll be needing help, real help.*

*. . . bronchitis—shades of you when you first came out here.*

*Naturally I worry about the children.*

Scary, the sound of this.

More than scary.

"Family, after all, is family." Lally, swallowing the last
mouthful left among her ice cubes, sent mental apologies to
her niece Joan.

Joan did not live in Carmel, in case someone might be interested enough to make inquiries about her well-being. She
lived in Savannah, Georgia, *was* divorced, *did* have two boys,
enjoyed gleaming health, and was on the brink of a promising
marriage to a man of Savannah fortune and family.

But there was nothing to stop Joan-from-Carmel writing
letters of increasing despair.

Just to let young Darrell, bless him, see—for his own good
—that from here on in it was not a matter of "when" but a
matter of "if."

Darrell abruptly switched the subject. "I called two radio
stations a while back. Nothing, but I'll try some more this
afternoon."

"Why not wait until Monday? People in the better-paid
professions have a way of drifting off early on Friday afternoons." She smiled warmly on him. "In the meantime, I
don't like to pry but you must have spent a good deal flying
out here. Suppose I write a little check so you can cash it
before three and have some green folding money on you."

He was pleased if a little embarrassed; he hadn't decided

how to go about asking for a small loan. But there was also a trace of worry. She had always seemed to him a consistent kind of person. Different now, first hounding him about work and then openhanded and amiable. Was she getting a bit odd, scatty, at her age? Blowing hot one minute and cold the next?

A poor lookout, especially considering the troubles of her niece Joan.

He got up and, noticing a restlessness about him, she said, "You're not to consider yourself housebound. You can take the car and cash your check, you'll remember where my bank is. And while you're up there will you pick me up a loaf of rye bread, unsliced, at the bakery? It's new, next door to the bank."

She went to get her handbag, which was hanging by its strap from the kitchen doorknob. She wrote a check and gave it to him.

Seventy-five dollars. Not bad at all.

"Thanks a lot, Lally. I'll pay you back of course."

"Before you go, would you mind . . . ? I'm very good with haircutting scissors. I always did Tom's."

He submitted with a good grace. "But no skinhead stuff, please."

"No, a nice loose bell. Just to mid-nape and the bottom of your earlobes. You have very attractive hair." She did her clipping at speed, having spread a newspaper under the kitchen chair. Finishing, she gave the top of his head a pat, a kind instinctive pat.

He looked nervously into the little splashed round mirror over the sink and was relieved. He looked okay, in fact better than usual.

She got out the car keys for him. "I'll expect you when I see you. Lunch is free-lance around here, make anything you want when you want it. The round garden looks like Kew now, gorgeous job."

He cashed the check at her bank in the shopping center on North Fourth Street, bought the loaf of unsliced rye, and then stood considering outside the bakery.

On his last trip out, he had found a little bar three or four blocks from here, nice tacky place that served sandwiches too, a dark cool escape from the sun. Not the kind of hostelry Lally was likely to go into, ever.

It would be pleasant to get out of the sun. The broad road was scathed in its relentless sunny glare, no trees along it to rest the eyes and reassure the spirit. At least half the heavy noontime traffic consisted of pickup trucks, often with a dog on board.

He parked the Pontiac in the small lot at the rear of the bar, which was called JoJo's. Six booths along one side, a bar along the other, fourteen or fifteen customers, a not offensive smell of frying onions.

Darrell sat at the far end of the bar, and in no mood to throw his store of cash around asked the thin dark bartender for a glass of draft beer and—scanning the painted menu board over the bar—a cheese sandwich on whole wheat bread, no butter, please, plenty of mustard.

When his lunch was served, he asked the bartender what he'd like and got a happy surprised look: this was evidently not the ordinary way of the world at JoJo's. "A whiskey with something to wet it, okay?" the man asked, and drank from a shot glass before drawing himself a glass of beer. "Cheers. Thanks. You new around here?" Soft Mexican or Spanish accent. He leaned his elbows on the bar, obviously open for conversation.

This was often interrupted by requests and refills for other patrons but Darrell was able to obtain in bits and pieces some useful and in ways astonishing information.

He explained that an uncle from Seattle was thinking of relocating here and wanted his nephew ("My name is Pete") to get him an idea of current real estate values. The part of Albuquerque he was interested in was the North Valley.

"Oh, now you're talking. I live close. My name in return is Rick. Rick Chavez."

"He once visited a friend on Andalusia Trail . . ."

"Forty an acre," Rick delivered promptly.

"Forty what?"

A lift of eyebrows over the dark sparkling eyes. "Not dollars, in case you . . . forty *thousand.*"

Darrell in a bemused fashion ate half his cheese sandwich and drank a third of his glass of beer.

Three minutes later, they resumed. "He'd want a house. Not big but not too small, good condition. He likes adobe. A garage too, not just a pull-in concrete place with a lid over it."

"Then I hope"—Rick's manner was courteous but doubtful —"that your uncle is a well-off man. For instance, there's a place on Del Rio, in the Valley, I know of. The house isn't much to look at, not even adobe, three acres, and they're asking two hundred and twenty-seven thousand for it. They may or may not get that, but the way land's selling here . . . so you can see." He spread his hands and grinned. "If he wants to spend even bigger money, there's always the Northeast Heights."

"Well, of course he could look there too. I'll keep asking around. He doesn't want to hand himself over to some steel-assed real estate dealer before he knows what he's getting into."

"You can't blame him." He added with a farewell smile as Darrell got off the barstool, "Lots of sharks swimming around here these days—biting off an arm here and a leg there."

## 7

"Any writing paper around?" Darrell asked. "I thought I'd better take care of that change of address before I forget."

Lally was reading a book in the living room, radio music on low, classical stuff. "Good idea. In the drawer of the desk there, and I think there's a stamp or two left."

He smiled at her. "I'm off to my room. I compose better in solitude, even a few sentences."

The New York duplex had been sublet for a period of at least two years while his parents would be living in Bonn. Jennifer, then. No bother to her, she'd just have her secretary forward his mail, if there was any.

But of course she'd notice the postmark. Take care of that.

"Dear Jennifer, I stopped here on the way out West (you know the saying, go West, young man, and I heard of something good in San Francisco)."

Here, automatic writing seemed to take over, guiding his ballpoint pen. He didn't really think his way from sentence to sentence, it just got put down on paper.

"I was shocked to see that Lally isn't at all well. She doesn't say what it is and I don't like to ask, afraid of some ghastly answer. She has these fits of very deep depression. So what I think I'll do is stay here for a bit and try to cheer her up. I have temporary work at a nice bar, so can save up to launch myself in Frisco. In the meantime I'm going to give your apartment as my mailing address, okay? And then please send on. When I'm off and on my way, Lally can then re-forward. Love, Darrell."

He reread this missive, folded it, and put it in the envelope. Well, what the hell. Why not? He had no fears that Jennifer would get on the phone to communicate with her dear Aunt Lally and see how she was. Any and all illnesses bored Jennifer. To her, Lally was next thing to a total stranger, probably not seen for fifteen years or so.

And Jennifer had more glamorous things to do with her time and her telephone than pursue rumors of ill health across two thousand miles.

No, she would sigh—briefly—with relief at the temporary bar job and the bright hopes in California. And the lovely distance that would separate him from the family.

He stamped the envelope and went out, put it in the mailbox on one side of the driveway, and returned to the living room. He wanted very badly to find out from Lally in casual conversation the extent of her land. One and a half acres times forty thousand dollars—or two, or three?

But he couldn't quite assemble the words, the easy lead-in. And if he were seen from a window pacing off the acreage on foot that wouldn't look very good.

Wait a minute. His variegated jobs had provided him with a wealth of odds-and-ends information not immediately available at everybody's fingertips. The County Assessor's Office ought to do nicely, as soon as he got around to it.

Lally looked up from her afternoon paper, the Albuquerque *Tribune*, which she had just opened.

"It seems there's to be a gathering of the clans," she said. "Or sort of."

"What clans?"

"Your brother Tony's due here in a few days to . . ."

"Jesus Christ," said Darrell, stopping as though he had been struck in the chest by a flung stone.

"Now, dear, really."

"What's he coming here for?"

"It says"—scanning her paper—"that they have to reshoot

a scene, several scenes and sequences, and don't want to have
to go all the way back to Spain. So he's heading here with his
camera crews and whatnot. It says he can find the right sce-
nery here and he wants a bit of mountain for some reason or
another."

"Why doesn't he go to Santa Fe? That's where all the Tony
Hydes go."

"Don't ask *me*. I don't know anything at all about the indus-
try. I never go to movies. I shock too easily, I suppose. I
believe the last movie I saw was *Orient Express*, ten years or so
back, because I'm fond of Agatha Christie. But I walked out
of that in the middle."

She smiled a little sourly. "He's certainly not coming here
so that he can pay a side visit to me. I haven't seen the boy, or
rather man, since Tom and I went East for your Grandmother Hyde's funeral. He was twelve or thirteen then.
Rather a stunning kid, as I look back."

Musingly, she went on, "Maybe he can dig up some work
for you as an extra."

Darrell wasn't going to go into that: no helping hands any
longer from the Hydes. And he wouldn't for a thousand dollars a day go begging to Tony for throwaway work.

"Oh, they'll bring all their own people with them. Union
rules and all that." Union rules probably didn't apply to ex-
tras but Lally had admitted her complete ignorance about
moviemaking.

She dropped the paper over an arm of her chair after a
glance at her watch. "I'm glad you brought the car back early.
I'd forgotten I made an appointment for three-thirty with my
lawyer."

Darrell found he was quite capable of feeling deep shock
right on the heels of plain shock.

"Your lawyer . . . ?" Ass. Shut up. Why should he sound
as if he cared or was curious about her visiting her lawyer?

"There was a question, it seems, about title to a little piece of land I bought on Candelaria Road," Lally said. "But I think he's got it cleared up, I just have to sign a couple of pieces of paper. For that little ceremony he will probably charge me twenty-five dollars. In addition to his title-clearing fees. What's the old saying—it costs money to make money? Well, it does."

For this legal visit, she changed into a brown cotton suit, ribbed lisle stockings, and brown brogues. Emerging from her bedroom into the living room, she saw Darrell's numbed gaze. "Do I have any ghosts around here? You look as if you'd just seen one. Or is it these funny stockings? Varicose veins," she explained. "Not bad for someone my age, but they show a bit through nylon. Will you stay here until I get back so we don't have to have an all-out lockup? I made some fresh banana ice cream while you were off, help yourself if you're hungry."

When the screen door closed behind her, Darrell allowed his facial muscles to sag a little.

Was the piece of land on Candelaria Road just a faked explanation? Was she really on her way to make a change in her will, maybe split the property between him and Joan, or even hand it all over to Joan?

If title to the land on Candelaria was in the process of being cleared, there was no way on earth of finding out the truth of the matter because it wouldn't yet be on record at the County Assessor's Office.

But . . . if there *was* extra, real true property . . . maybe not just this one place . . . ?

He had a sense of violent helplessness, of struggling while he was bound hand and foot. A very unpleasant feeling that hit him in the heart.

Action, any kind of action, would help. Now would be a good time to poke around a bit in desk drawers. Bankbooks and so on. Being careful not to leave the slightest appearance of any minor disturbance, any furtive search.

He pulled out the center desk drawer where he had gotten his writing paper.

What if she had forgotten something, and came back to the house for it? She had only been gone two or three minutes. Had she been carrying her handbag? He couldn't remember.

Leaving the drawer half open, he went nervously to the screen door and looked into the eyes of a girl directly outside, her knuckles, ready to knock, a few inches from the door-frame.

"Oh," she said in a startled way. "Lally out? You're Darrell, aren't you? We met years ago, I'm Lydia, Lydia Jerome."

She was a small slender girl with eyes of a curious beauty, a crystal-lit lavender, thickly black-lashed. Her dark hair was side-parted and fell to the edges of her delicate jawline. Her nose was short and straight and her mouth had a lilt and fineness to its cut but it was the eyes you noticed most of all.

After a pause just a few seconds too long, Darrell said, "She's gone off to her lawyer. But come on in. Yes, I do re-member you—the birthday party."

"I really just stopped to pick up a book I borrowed for her from the school library that she wants returned."

As they went into the living room, her eyes went, as Dar-rell's did, to the open desk drawer. Was there such a thing as a clang of silence?

"I was just getting out some writing paper," he said. "To write home, you know. East." He walked across the room, took out a sheet of paper, and closed the drawer firmly. He was aware of what must be a visible blush. But no, he'd got-ten a strong burn on his face this morning in the garden, thank God.

Guilt invented in his imagination a sentence or two, this girl to Lally: "It did look rather funny. The desk drawer open . . . and then he came to the door to look out through the screen . . ."

But she didn't give the impression of a peeking, sneaking,

gossipy kind of girl. She went to the bookshelves under the two side windows of the living room and pulled out a thick red-bound book.

School library? Did she still go to school—college? But people did these days, people he knew his age were still taking course after graduate course.

She put her hand into the pocket of her white linen blazer and took out bills and coins, which she laid on the coffee table. "Will you tell Lally this is the brandy money, returned?" Twenty-four dollars and seventy-five cents, two bottles. Was she a brandy freak? She certainly didn't look it.

With a smile, and "I hope you have a nice time here, Darrell," she left. As though observed by unseen eyes, he went to his bedroom with the sheet of writing paper and placed it on the desk with his pen beside it. Just in case. Just in case.

Going back through Tom's den, he paused a moment. A memory clicked. Was it still there?

On his twentieth anniversary with the firm of Boone and Boone, Tom's associates had presented him with a shotgun. Darrell had once seen it when he went to borrow a sweater from the closet, and in fourteen-year-old excitement had asked Lally about it.

She said Tom would never shoot anything to eat unless they were starving; and would never shoot *at* anyone except to save her life. "Probably wouldn't do it to save his own. It's not loaded—the ammunition they gave him is up there on the shelf. You can take it down and run your fingers over it if you like." It was, she told him, a 12-gauge Browning over-and-under shotgun. It was four feet long with a walnut stock.

He opened the closet door. The hanging bar and most of the side hooks were empty. There was a rack fixed to the wall at the back, holding two old umbrellas and the shotgun.

He lifted his eyes to the high shelf. The ammunition box was still there too.

The only shooting he had ever done was in amusement

arcades. His aim had turned out to be pretty good. In fact, very good.

Just as he was closing the door of the closet, he noticed in the light from a nearby window his own footprints in the film of dust on the hardwood floor of the closet.

God, what if he hadn't gotten that one accidental glance downward in the right light?

He went into the kitchen and took a dry mop from its place behind the door, mopped the closet floor thoroughly, and then so as not to draw notice to its dustlessness mopped the rest of the den floor around the edges of the worn Indian-looking rug. It was zigzag-striped in cream, slate blue, and henna color. (Could it be valuable?)

For further authenticity, he mopped the floor of his own room. "This is a kingdom of dust, this place," Lally had complained long ago. "No sooner have you finished swiping it off than it's back on all your surfaces again, that eternal red dust. Especially when the wind's blowing."

If he were found at this domestic task—but surely she wouldn't have finished her business with her lawyer this soon?—the impression on her part could only be a good one.

Helpful Darrell, improving the shining hour.

The devil finds work for idle hands.

## 8

The weekend brought Darrell's spirits bounding back, at least temporarily. Nothing catastrophic in the way of business dealings, lawyers and so on, could happen on weekends, could it? There was a suspension in time to be enjoyed to the full.

Enjoyed even though, this Saturday morning at eight-thirty, the winds blew. He had forgotten the feel of them, in the way you tend to forget maddening things about which you can do nothing. With a comfortable breakfast of raised buckwheat cakes, quantities of butter and maple syrup, and Canadian bacon inside him, he went out into the blast and express-train sound of the force in the cottonwoods. Dust from the edges of the asphalted road followed him in a tan haze, dust you could taste in your mouth.

He found an outer wall of one of the gardens facing north to offer him blessed protection. There he sat on the ground in refuge, the sun blazing on him.

He fell into the most pleasant landowner's reveries, gazing about him.

That great meadow, now. One thing that could be done with it was to plant it to grapevines. There were, he had read in the evening paper, a few faint beginnings of turning Albuquerque and its vicinity into wine country. Take the old apple trees in the center down, or leave them for romantic effect. Have his own winery, his own little bottling plant, his own label. Maybe the two apple trees on it . . . no, that would suggest cider. Hyde's Fine Wines. Hyde's Fine Estate-Bottled Wines.

Or, say, devote the space to a health club. Olympic-size swimming pool in the center, jogging track around it, horses to ride. Hyde's Health, Inc. Every hour seemed to produce more fitness nuts. Well, it had always been a good idea to live in your own times and hoist the gold out of them.

And then he thought in astonishment, I'm thinking like my father, or Tony. Or Roger, or Jennifer.

A third possibility, if he decided against fine wines and health, was to sell the parcel of property instead. But first plant it attractively. A cloud of Russian olive trees at one side. They grew fast and made a delightful silvery-green cool blur in the hot mountainscape.

The mountains. He recalled from Lally's letters that snow usually fell predictably on them from toward the end of November on. The unquestionably healthy joys of skiing, downhill and cross-country, and coming home feeling like a million dollars to a leaping fire and—why not?—a hot buttered rum.

Lally, rounding a corner of the garden wall, said, "You look pleased with life, young Darrell."

"You know how much I like it here."

"Well, sorry to interrupt your communings with nature but I just got a call from the bishop. Lydia's father, that is. She told him you were interested in finding work out here—I had told *her*. Now, this would only be a quickie job, a greenhouse he wants assembled and then planted, perhaps a little plumbing work to go with it. But it would give you some working capital."

Darrell was not only mildly alarmed at the prospect of labor thrust immediately on him, but also extremely confused.

"Church work for a bishop? To grow flowers for the altar or something?"

"No, no, that's just my name for him, the bishop—and a

spoiled selfish bishop into the bargain. You'll see what I mean when you meet him. He wants to describe the job to you this morning and hopes you'll be able to start Monday. I think it's part curiosity, his wanting to see you right away—he lives a very retired life. You can take the car. I'll make a little map for you, it's not more than a mile or so from here."

Twenty minutes later he parked the Pontiac in front of the Jerome house. It was on Rio Grande Boulevard, at a corner where a little lane ran off toward the mountains. The high surrounding walls and what little could be seen of the house were adobe, the walls not forbidding but warm and rich in the sunlight. Great cottonwoods embraced the house, he saw when he went through the arch in the wall, the gate wide open. There were more arches on the enclosed porch, which was painted an agreeable ghostly blue-gray.

He thought it was an attractive house, two stories to it, and immediately found himself wondering if it would bring more on the open market than his. Than Lally's. Depended a good deal on how much land went with it, of course.

He was climbing the porch steps when the blue-gray door opened. Lydia said, "Good morning, Darrell." She wore a pink shirt and raspberry-red linen shorts, and a businesslike bibbed white apron which came to mid-shin. "I'll take you right in." As though, it sounded, to some sort of Presence.

His impression was correct. In the living room opening off the left side of the hall, a room swimming in sun and wind-shivered leaf shadow, sat a large stout man; or rather half lay, in a tilted leather reclining chair. His broad heavy face with its high Roman forehead was a rich rose color. His eyes were blandly blue. He was bald except for a ruffly band of gray hair worn in the manner of a wreath.

On the table at his side was a crystal decanter full of a hazel-brown liquid, a glass, and several bottles of pills and capsules. A heavy, knobby black walking stick was propped against one arm of his chair. He wore—to Darrell's astonishment—a knicker suit of cream-colored linen, and cream-colored knee socks. Where in God's name would you find a knicker suit these days?

He put out a large well-formed hand for Darrell to shake. Lydia started to say, "This is—" and he waved her impatiently off. "Darrell Hyde, whom else did I expect this morning? Please bring us coffee in ten minutes."

She went out, closing the door behind her. Dismissed. Old bastard, Darrell thought. How does she stand him? In this day and age?

The bishop (no, don't start that or he might say it out loud) removed the top of his decanter and poured himself an inch and a half. A waft reached Darrell's nose. The brandy money hereby explained.

"I won't offer you any, you're young and healthy, obviously. Whereas I . . ." He sighed. "But one bears these things. Take that comfortable ottoman close by, my hearing's not all that it should be."

Darrell found himself in effect sitting at Percival Jerome's uplifted feet, which were clad in cordovan leather slippers.

"And now to business, dear boy." The voice was sonorous and exact in its shaping of syllables. "I like good work, you know, neat and true throughout." He explained that he had ordered and was now in receipt of a disassembled greenhouse, which he would like placed on the back wall of the house. Extra shelving would be required; not nearly enough shelves had been supplied. "When it's up and in place, we will see what else we want in the way of hose connections, a center table or stand for flower arranging, and so on."

Lydia came in with a tray bearing a flowered china pot of coffee, flowered cups and saucers, cream and sugar. She put this down on the lamp table on the other side of the invalid's reclining chair and with a faint smile at Darrell removed herself.

"Now then, what do you charge for labor? Plain simple

labor, nothing—mmm—creative required. Will you pour our coffee? Just a touch of cream in mine, one lump of sugar."

Darrell obeyed. "I'd like to have a look at the thing first, how complicated it is, and the space where it's to go, then I'll give you an estimate."

"An estimate!" The bishop, or rather Jerome, raised his eyebrows. "Now we're beginning to sound like high finance." He laughed rumblingly. "Just a matter, you know, of inserting slot A into slot B. Lydia could do it but she has an absolute incomprehension of putting things together. All thumbs."

Good for you, Lydia, Darrell thought. He drank his coffee, which was very hot and very good. A tiny alarm went off in Jerome's watch and he said, "Time for my capsule. Do go find Lydia and have her show you the elements of your little task."

The broad center hall of the house went through to the back, where there was a heavy clear glass and screening combination door. Good idea, he thought in his landowner's frame of reference. In winter you could pull the second glass panel at the bottom up over the screen and have floods of winter sunlight in the house. Ought to cut heating costs too.

The back lawn was deep, neatly mown, extending to its high adobe wall. There were three magnificent cottonwoods flinging wild windy light across the green. Lydia was under a tree near the wall, picking white and pale blue iris from a long border. She struck him suddenly as a natural inhabitant of swimming light and shadow, a delicate wood creature, or unassuming unnamed wildflower found deep in moss by a brook in a forest.

As he approached her, he thought that some comment on her parent seemed in order, as they'd just met. But nothing polite and neutral—much less complimentary—came to mind. So instead he said abruptly, "Nice morning. That library book—are you taking college courses?"

"No, I teach at Miss Withington's. It's a private girls' school." White and blue from the iris reflected up onto her throat and cheekbones.

"Teach what?"

"Art."

"Are you an artist, then?"

"An occasional dabble."

"Do you sell at all?"

"Enough to run this house for possibly three and a half days."

So it was her salary that put food on the table and kept Jerome in brandy and cream linen knicker suits.

His curiosity heightened. "What did your father do before he was . . . incapacitated?"

"He was a lawyer, an expert on financial law. He often worked with Boone and Boone, which is how I got to know Lally."

Thinking of his summonings and dismissings of this girl, Darrell said before he could stop himself, "How do you stand the old—I mean, how do you stand him?" He was horrified at this question asked of a stranger. Or no, not really a stranger.

She smiled, a tilted smile. "Well, short of putting poison in his brandy—" And then, severely correcting herself, "Lally may have told you my mother left him flat after twenty years of marriage. He's not well, not capable of working, and he hasn't a handsome private income or much of *any* private income. So there you are."

"I'm sorry, I didn't mean to butt in." He was deeply embarrassed. "Does your land end with this wall?"

"Yes. It's only a quarter of an acre, but helpful in the matter of taxes, when they come due."

"*Taxes!*" said Darrell in a voice of startled horror. Not an owner of anything, he had forgotten that you had to pay tribute to someone for what was entirely yours.

"Yes. As in death and. Why are we talking about death and

taxes when I should be showing you the greenhouse, or
rather the slabs and bits and pieces and nuts and bolts?"

The greenhouse was not to be freestanding, but to go up
against the outer wall of the kitchen, which had two large
deep arched windows facing south. It would be about the size
of his small bedroom at Lally's, ten feet by ten.

Four big paper cartons, opened, stood by the back door.
Lydia pulled from her shorts pocket the pamphlet which had
arrived with these and Darrell studied diagrams and instruc-
tions. He wondered if this large unnecessary toy had come
out of her own pocket too. Or did Jerome get Social Security,
and maybe had a small bank account?

"Just tell me what it will cost and I'll pass it along later.
His capsule makes him drowsy sometimes."

"My usual work charge is six dollars an hour, for jobs like
assembling. After that we can talk about what else is needed."

After a slight hesitation, he asked, "Who's to be the gardener? You? In addition to running the house and teaching
school and bringing hot coffee when it's ordered?"

"My father . . . at first." Was there a trace of weariness
under the amiable irony? "His doctor says he can't sit in that
chair all day and needs some sort of puttering exercise for an
hour every afternoon. The wall border's too heavy a job, a
hands-and-knees job, and he doesn't care for walking,
so . . ."

"Well, I'll be off. I'll be here Monday morning. When do
you leave for school so that I don't have to get him out of his
chair?"

"Eight-thirty."

"Okay." He hesitated. "You'd know if . . . is there a decent art supply store around here?"

She looked interested. "Do you paint or what?"

"In your words, only an occasional dabble. Only, small-
scale sculpture." Christ, now he was really committing himself, sooner or later she would, if only in politeness, want to

see what he was doing with his sculpting. But the question, and the desire, had risen unannounced from somewhere at the back of his mind.

The last thing he had ever shaped in clay with his hands was a lion, when he was nine years old. He was going to model a lion cub to go with it when his brother Tony, who was five years older, reached out a hand and with his thumb, for fun, shoved the face and the muzzle deep into the mane.

"Darby's is the nearest, Second Street near Osuna."

"Thanks. See you."

He drove to Darby's and bought for a beginning ten pounds of modeling clay. If his clay needed supports—was armatures the word?—he could make them out of wire clothes hangers.

He felt strange as he drove home, stirred up and excited, confused and a little alarmed.

Where was he really *headed?* What was he about to start on? Start on . . .

That conversation with Lydia. Death. Death and taxes. "Short of putting poison in his brandy . . ." Did she know he was Lally's heir? Very possibly. Did she know he was broke, and wandering, and had been for years? Maybe, maybe not; Lally wouldn't have put it exactly that way even to a close friend. Or would she?

Did she, Lydia, leading the life she did under the encumbrance and demands of her father, possess the same talent as he, the ability to read people deep under surfaces?

Watch yourself, under those comprehending lavender eyes.

Watch yourself very carefully.

## 9

Lydia wanted late-afternoon light for her watercolor sketch of Lally's slated yard and juniper tree and stand of iris, and on this Saturday at six sat on her folding canvas stool at the edge of the road, happily lost in work. Her father never dined until seven-thirty, holding that any earlier hour was for the commonplace, so that she had time to spare. But then, you didn't dither over a watercolor, the wet airy transparent medium demanded speed.

Behind her she heard a perfectly ordinary sound, rubber bicycle tires on the asphalt of the road. Intent on an iris, she didn't lift her head until the bicycle stopped right behind her. She was aware of its being leaned against the low wall.

A tall man in his mid-thirties was the rider. He came around to face her and said, "Am I right for Mrs. Thomas Hyde?" He was a man of splendid looks. Thick dark hair, commanding nose, large brilliant dark eyes under heavy, absolutely straight brows. He wore white duck pants, a dark violet shirt with the sleeves rolled up, and graceful thong sandals. Over one shoulder was hooked a heather-colored pearl-buttoned linen jacket.

There was something familiar about him, even though she knew she had never laid eyes on him before. Something familiar about his voice too, richly resonant, at ordinary pitch but you could feel it coursing against your skin and muscles.

"Yes, this is her house."

He took a step or two to look down over her shoulder. "That's very nice. May I buy it when it's finished? Unless

your iris petals run into your slates." Nothing condescending
about the opinion, the offer. It occurred to her, though, to
wonder if he was a little drunk, or on some urbane drug; or
perhaps his eyes always held that hypnotic dark sparkle.

As if in answer, he said, "I've been partying for hours, a
mile or so down the road, and it suddenly came to me in mid-
swallow that I had a long-lost aunt practically at arm's length
away. So I borrowed a bicycle and here I am."

Yes, there was a slippage in a syllable here and there, explained by the partying.

"An aunt?" She was too bemused to get it straight.

"My name is Hyde too, Tony Hyde."

"Oh . . . do I connect you with the movies?"

"I hope so." He put his hand on the top of her head and
laughed. "Naughty girl!"

"And . . ." Not very nice, to Darrell, to have the relationship as a second mention. "Darrell's brother?"

"Yes. One of two of them."

Lally, hearing the voices outside, came to the screen door.
Who was that with Lydia? Surely it wasn't . . . She opened
the door a little. Tony turned his head and went swiftly
across the slates. He pulled the door wide open, came in, and
gave her an enormous powerful hug.

"My God, how many years has it been? And is Lally kin-
dergarten or nursery for Alice? I always wondered. And may
I pay you a visit or are you just on your way somewhere? And
who is that captured wood nymph out in front? Not, I hope, a
blood relative of mine, which would be hampering."

Lally felt as though a collection of fireworks had been let
off in her usually quiet hall.

There wasn't, as with Darrell, an invitation to the kitchen
for a drink. She was unused to this feeling of fluster and
didn't quite know how to handle it.

"How nice, how . . . wonderful to see you, Tony, I'd read

you were on your way here. In the papers. Do come into the
. . ."

He was too marvelously put together, altogether too lumi-
nously full of himself, for the shabby flowery living room.
His eyes went everywhere, taking, raking it in, and back to
her to do the same.

He made her feel untidy, and old, and tongue-tied. Well—
putting a hand to her wind-scrambled hair—she *was* untidy.
And old, although she had never thought much about that
before. And not very practiced in swift easy chitchat. But
these film people of course were never at a loss for words.

"Sit down, I'll just go and—what can I bring you in the
way of drink? And no, I'm not on my way anywhere, I'm
delighted that you dropped in." She paused, trying to get
back her balance. Trying to get back her*self?* "Yes, Lally is a
nickname for Alice. The girl out in front is Lydia Jerome, a
young friend. She likes to paint right on the scene, and
mostly when she sets up her work outside other people's
houses or gardens they get suspicious and think she's casing
the house for a robbery or some such thing—" Stop talking.

"Would a cup of tea be too much trouble? I've been on
various refreshments most of the day, down the road . . .
and do you think you could persuade that bed of violets out
there to transplant herself in here to join us?"

When Lally went to put the request, Lydia said, "In a few
minutes. I'm almost finished. He—your nephew—has taken it
into his head that he wants to buy it. Is he all right, do you
think?"

"You mean, sober?" Here, briefly free of her guest, with
Lydia helping her to regain her composure, Lally added, "At
least that's the polite old-fashioned word when one is discuss-
ing people under the influence of things. I don't know him
that well, or at all, to say what his normal manner is. But do
hurry."

"Where's Darrell—can't he help?"

For some reason it had never occurred to Lally to inform the man in the living room that Darrell was staying here. Had he come, after all, to see his brother, and not her? But he hadn't so far even mentioned the name.

She went straight back to the kitchen, made a pot of tea, and fixed for her own refreshment a short drink of scotch and water. What a nuisance tea for a stranger was, an elegant stranger. Somewhere she had linen napkins, but where? And there were shiny rings left by glasses on the brass tray, wipe it clean. She brushed a spider out of a teacup, rinsed it, dried it, and went to the mirror over the sink to try to tidy her hair with her hands.

Would he expect a thin cucumber or watercress sandwich along with his tea? Too bad, she hadn't either available.

Changing a saucer with a chipped edge for an intact one, she thought with horror, What if he has concluded, not unnaturally, that he will be asked for dinner? Or even to stay the night?

People who were dazzlingly accomplished, high flyers, people on—what was the expression?—fast tracks, were terribly unnerving, exhausting, to have around the house.

In the living room, pouring his tea, she asked, "Were you stopping by to see Darrell?"

"Darrell?" He raised his eyebrows and said in the tone of one who is secretly bent on amusing only himself, "Darrell's in Rockport, in Massachusetts, doing something or other in the yacht line."

From the door of the dining room, leading into the hall, Darrell heard this. He stopped and stood, hardly breathing.

He had gone, half an hour before, across the field toward the far band of trees, still in search of visible property boundaries. A tumbledown old fence, perhaps, somewhere deep in the trees, or old white stone markers. He found nothing, but the sweet resinous odor of sun-blazed pines kept him wandering for a time, among boles that went from slender to old and thick.

He almost forgot what he was looking for, he felt so well and happy and caught up in dreams that weren't really dreams at all.

Now, standing in the dining-room doorway, he wanted to turn and run. He might have, except that Lydia came in at the front door opposite him, her watercolor block carefully balanced on the palms of her hands, an odd look on her face, a sort of radiance. Was it her painting that had made her so happy?

She laid the block of paper down on the old carved chest to the right of the door, and said, "I'm not pursuing you about greenhouses, I was trying to get the light on Lally's iris and slate."

Escape hatch closed. They went together into the living room, where Lally was saying, ". . . was in Rockport, yes, but he's on his way out to . . . Oh, there you are, Darrell. And Lydia."

What a relief, not to have to be alone any longer with Tony Hyde. But she hadn't been able to take her eyes off him. Unworldly in her ways as she was, she somehow knew that all his throwaway-casual clothing had cost a great deal of money. Indeed, he himself looked as if he had cost a great deal of money.

Tony showed neither surprise nor particular interest at his brother's entrance. "What happened?" he asked. "Did your yacht sink?" Adding in the same secretly amused way, "Again?"

Darrell thought for a panicky second or two about his letter to Jennifer, hinting at some possible mortal illness hanging over Lally. But, forget it, Tony and Jennifer probably didn't meet more than once a year or so, and besides, they disliked each other.

He wanted to think of a quick, crisp, and rude answer to

Tony's yacht question, but none came. He opened his mouth and closed it.

Lally said hastily, "Drinks for the two of you, I'll get them."

Tony, who had stood up at Lydia's entrance, came over and took her hand and led her to the chair he had been sitting in. "I'll take your arm, if I may. Your chair arm, that is. For the moment."

"Thank you," Lydia said, and still with that betraying light on her face, broke what had only been a long thirty seconds of silence. "Where were you doing your partying?"

"The Castletons. Friends of friends. Maybe you know them?"

"No, I don't. But they're well named. That colossal house of theirs . . . but . . ." A look of distress darkened her lavender eyes. "Wasn't one of their children drowned a couple of weeks ago? In their swimming pool?"

"Yes, the nurse or nanny or whatever was up to here in cocaine. Naturally the more people around, the more fun and games, the less they're apt to brood about it. In fact"—patting his breast pocket—"I took a note or so when nobody was looking. Move it back five or six centuries. Spain. A Moorish castle, a very young princeling, a nurse who is in the clutches or employ of . . . and one of those great formal pools, marble fretwork, cypresses and wandering peacocks and so on . . ."

"It's nice that any old horror is grist to your mill," Darrell interrupted harshly.

Tony gave him a savage brilliant smile. "Did anyone object when El Greco and a lot of other chaps decided to paint the crucified Christ?"

"I'm glad to see you rank yourself in such eminent company," Darrell said. He got up and left the room.

Lally and he nearly collided outside the door, she carrying

in one hand a crystalline martini for Lydia and a scotch for him. Bathroom, Lally concluded.

In a soft, measured way, Tony was saying, "That little . . . no-good . . . nowhere . . . nothing . . . sonofa—" The words cut off by Lydia's instinctively lifted fingers against his mouth.

Hardly knowing what she was saying, "You shouldn't. Nobody should." She felt the flash of weapons and the drip of blood. Uncomfortably heightened perceptions, perhaps, induced by this man's presence. She had never been so closely exposed to male power, beauty, and talent. To say nothing of the searchlight of his attention on her. Shock, or several kinds of shock, numbed her.

"Heavens," Lally said in an uncertain voice.

"Nothing heavenly about it." Tony got off the chair arm to pour more hot tea into his cup. "Families. They sometimes talk very frankly to each other, as you know. Sorry to blister the air of your living room. And Lydia's ears. Do you think you could spare me just a sip of that martini, Lydia?"

Darrell walked at a fast pace down Andalusia Trail, not going anywhere, just going away. The wind was dying but the air was still hazed with tan dust and he had a choking sensation in his throat. Poor kid. Poor Lydia. Poor child.

He'd have to tell her, unless this was just a half-hour segment of the Tony Hyde Revue: his inability to meet any reasonably attractive young woman without wanting to charm her into his back pocket.

If Tony was going to be here for more than four or five days he would have to tell her. That is, if Tony kept it up, after this one late-afternoon first meeting.

Tell her about the two wives tossed into the past . . . and some of the innumerable and occasionally messy affairs people he knew enjoyed telling him about . . . and that wretched girl who . . . or maybe it was just gossip, but . . .

This was no time to be walking away from someone who might be walking straight into trouble. He turned and started back.

When he got to Lally's house, the bicycle was gone.

## 10

Lally woke earlier than usual to grapple with whatever worry had been riding darkly through her dreams.

Tony. Did he talk that way to everybody, except aunts or pretty women? Or was that special soft frightening contempt reserved for spit-upon people—for Darrell, among them?

"That little . . . no-good . . . nowhere . . . nothing . . ." For this among her other reasons, she must press on, in her campaign to put Darrell squarely on his own two feet. Press on and bear down. Sympathy and kindness could open holes for people to sink into.

She got up at her usual six-thirty and dressed, shoving her shirttails into the elastic waist of her chambray pants with the speed and carelessness of someone half her age. Work to be done, no point in putting on fresh Sunday clothes, although in her case all that amounted to was her yellow and white striped cotton dress and newish yellow sandals.

She drank her first cup of hot powerful coffee, which she made with chicory, not to stretch coffee and save money but because she liked the aromatic tang. She went out into the gardens for her private invariable early-morning tour, when they offered dew along with every other wonder, color and texture and scent, because while even at this hour the sun was hot the early June mountain nights were still chilly. She eyed a dew-diamonded spiderweb in a wall corner and said to herself, oh, let it be, it's pretty in this light.

There was another small disturbance to try to shake off in the gardens: Lydia. On the one hand, it might do her good, even a short spin of high-powered attention from a remark-ably attractive *(looking)* man. On the other . . .

Lydia didn't talk much about it but Lally thought she had lost at least one promising partner because of the bishop. Not only could Percy be, to put it mildly, insolent to people he didn't warmly welcome in the Jerome house. But there was the much realer, larger problem: Lydia and any mate must manage the funds to provide some kind of daily and possibly nightly care for him if and when his daughter took her depar-ture. And at the price of health care at home these days . . . and he wouldn't settle for some poor, kind Chicano woman who might have to bring along a child or two . . .

She had no idea of the exact name and nature of his illness, or how much of it was real and how much self-induced. Like many people of open if skeptical mind, she could form no sententious judgments on how much the mind and emotions affected the body and vice versa. Perhaps, because of the busi-ness of his wife walking off, he was determined that under no circumstances would he lose the close and forever concern of the only other Jerome, his daughter. Or perhaps he might have something just plain horrible and didn't want it known by anybody except his doctor.

She had been around this mental route again and again, and always ended up as she did now, baffled. The mysterious invalid was an unfortunate commonplace in all too many families. Leave it at that.

Darrell was pouring himself coffee when she went back into the kitchen. He had a scrubbed, showered look to him and was wearing a shirt she hadn't seen before, tattersall, good-looking, with immaculate chinos.

Maybe family competition is good for you, young Darrell, Lally thought. She cooked the Sunday breakfast which Tom had liked best, top round steak pan-fried in butter, broiled tomatoes, and toasted English muffins.

Cutting into her steak, she said, "You'll be working tomorrow, why not just laze today? Me, I'm going to roll up my sleeves and begin tackling the apartment. I feel in my bones it's going to be needed not in any distant future."

Because he disliked the subject so much, Darrell bent over backward, verbally. "Can't I help you? It's heavy work."

"Later on. First I have to face the files, God help me."

Six years ago, Boone and Boone had gone abruptly out of business. The brothers were in their sixties. One of them had disappeared with all the firm's holdings and a young filing clerk named Dora. The other had promptly had a heart attack and died. There were no takers for this rather overshadowed house of business and in a last spurt of efficiency the elderly secretary, Miss Minns, took care of closing the offices and disposing of their contents.

To Lally, she had said over the phone, "I'm sending you Mr. Hyde's files, no one ever used his office after his demise. Just in case some question from a client or the IRS might crop up some year, you never know."

The files had been dollied up the stairway at the back of the garage. Lally had never approached them. She had a dread of printed forms of any kind and hated figures, additions and subtractions and multiplications. Involved pieces of paper with lines to be filled in seized her with deep depression.

But now, no help for it. Going up the stairs, she decided to be quick about the job, ruthless. Nobody could take her to court for throwing the stuff away, could they? As far as she knew there was no law on the books about widows having to hold their husbands' business papers.

And in the course of the past six years there had not been one single inquiry from a client or the IRS or anybody at all.

The metal files, which had been stacked in fours, breast-high, in the office, had been separated into stacks of two each for moving purposes. Dear God, how many?—sixteen filing drawers in all.

She had brought up a large empty paper carton to serve as

what would be the first of many wastebaskets. She had also put on thick socks and sneakers, as spider guards.

Well, don't just stand here staring at the horrible task waiting. She was out to help Darrell, there was point and purpose in a reverse sort of way to all this work. Although, in fact, the idea of the forlorn niece and her poor little fatherless boys had become almost real. In any case, why not clean it up, rent it out, and pocket the money? More for Darrell when her time came, or ended.

Keys to the files, neatly lettered for alphabetical identification, were in a little plastic bag taped to one of the drawer handles.

The wind rattled the windows in their frames. She unlocked and pulled out the drawer of the file nearest her foot. There was a scutter and a black widow spider—unmistakable, the round shining black bead high on thready straight legs— began to crawl at speed down the front of the drawer. She got it with her sneaker. Grim as its legend was, the bite of the black widow could usually cause death only in the very small and young. But to any victim of any age they contributed distressing muscular spasms and pain, and the bitten had no choice but to head straight for the doctor.

Reluctantly, she pulled her gardening gloves out of her pocket and put them on. Awkward to sort things with gloves on, but too chancy without them. And was she going to sort? Or just grab handfuls and throw them into the carton.

A compromise would be to spot-check here and there, to see if the records, the papers, looked dead and gone, belonging only to the dusty past. What would there be besides income tax forms of which Tom would hold the triplicate copy? Business audits? Correspondence? He seldom talked to her about his work because he knew it bored her.

But, looking down at the neatly serried papers—the file nearest to her went from M through P—she felt a silent upward breathing from them, private lives, the intimacies of personal finances, things that people usually liked to keep to themselves.

She was seldom nervous, but she was now. An unpleasant job when you looked it right in the face. Suppose some frantic woman, someone her age, came wailing to the door, "But I lost my [some vital document] and Mr. Hyde had the only copy of it."

She straightened her back uncertainly. Was that the sound of a footstep below? She had left the apartment door open and now she went to peer out and across the stair railing. Darrell was standing very quietly in the open doorway of the garage, his shadow long and dark on the concrete floor with the sun behind him.

"Darrell?"

He started, visibly, and looked up with a strange expression on his face, abstracted, closed. The expression rapidly vanished.

"I thought I'd just check and see if you wanted help after all."

"No, you're under orders, as I said, to laze." She turned and went back to M through P.

Darrell was telling the truth; he had been on the point of offering help. But, just at the door, his glance fell on the wooden handrail of the stairway. A memory surfaced, a paperback somebody had left on the seat of a bus going from Burlington to Pittsfield, Massachusetts. Though he was not a reader of mystery fiction—his interest lying mainly in history —he picked up the book to pass the time.

Someone had wanted to get rid of a rich grandmother who was about to change her will and leave all her money to the Humane Society because they had found and returned her Pekingese, lost for two weeks. The grandson paid her a visit at her country house in Tarrytown. In the course of the visit, he fastened a near-transparent slender nylon cord across the second step from the top of the long stairway leading to the ground floor. Grandmother had as usual risen from her bed in the morning, dressed, and started down to breakfast. Crash. Screams. Blood. Servants coming running. All over but the funeral. Grandson slips up the steps in panicky fruitless quest of a bottle of smelling salts and neatly whips cord from its moorings and pockets it.

Darrell never found out what happened after that because at Cheshire, north of Pittsfield, a man got on and sat down in the empty seat beside him. Snapping open a miniature chessboard, he asked without preamble, "Care for a game?"

Darrell abandoned grandmother and her murderer. He was good at chess.

Leaving the garage, he returned to a subject which had been occupying his mind a good deal: not stairways but sculpture.

It was still too early to call Jerome, who looked as if he had a talent for good sound sleep and plenty of it. Wait until near noon.

He took a five-mile round-trip walk along Andalusia Trail, feeling through the wind-whip the sun burning steadily into his skin. Going past a small dressy-looking brick shopping center, he paused before the windows of a men's clothing store.

Something white, as he was turning amazingly brown so soon. Not that he gave a damn about clothes, but . . .

He went in and bought a boat-necked fisherman's sweater of crunchy white knitted cotton, marked down from twenty to ten dollars, and a white belt of heavy webbing.

At eleven-thirty, he called the Jerome house. Lydia answered. "May I speak to the . . . to your father?" Darrell asked, after they had exchanged greetings. He remembered that there was a telephone, probably an extension, along with the pill bottles on one of Jerome's chairside tables.

"Good morning," Jerome came on plummily.

Plunge, don't dither. "The moment I met you, sir"—yes, "sir" seemed to be the ticket—"I thought how much I'd like to do a portrait bust of you."

"Great heavens. A *portrait* bust? Are you, then, a sculptor whose fame has not yet reached my ears?"

"Not all that well known, I'm afraid. An exhibition here and there, not one-man of course, a few pieces commissioned and sold. But yours would be done because of the . . . the challenge, no money involved."

"Well . . ." There was astonished pleasure in Jerome's voice. "I don't know . . . honored, I may say . . . as a young man I was painted in oils by Brewman Fane, who came to an unfortunate early death in Venice . . ."

"I'd like to make a start this afternoon, preliminary photographs and so on, study the best angles, you know." He thought that Jerome probably didn't know at all, which was a help.

"I like speed. I like firmness. I like application to a project in hand," said Jerome in solemn applause. "I'll have Lydia wake me from my nap before you get here, unless you care to name a time now?"

"No, a few little things to get out of the way first."

He went out to the garage and called to Lally, "I'm borrowing the car for ten minutes or so, all right? I need a roll of film. Is there anything you want picked up?"

The answering call, "No, nothing. The car's yours all day if you want it, I'm not going anywhere but crazy."

When he got back, and was in the kitchen making a sandwich for his lunch, Swiss cheese and sliced tomatoes on her fresh rye bread, she joined him. She washed her dusty hands at the sink and put the wet heels of her palms against her eyes. "Three drawers cleared out, anyway. Would you believe that the people next door, where the old tires are—the Martinezes—paid eleven thousand dollars in income taxes not so many years back? And I thinking they didn't have one cent to rub against the other."

"Maybe the tires are packed with heroin or some other goodie in that line," Darrell said.

They were having cinnamon cookies and coffee when the telephone rang. Lally took the call next door in Tom's office. Darrell listened hard.

"Hello, Tony, how are you? . . . Oh, yes. Rio Grande Boulevard, I don't remember the number as I never mail anything to Lydia, but it's at the corner of Felice Lane, high walls, blue porch, adobe . . . Yes, hope to see you soon." A pause and then, "Goodbye."

Coming back, she reported, "He says not to tell her that he might drop over this afternoon, he wants to take her by surprise. Myself, I don't care for that kind of surprise."

Darrell merely shrugged and then asked if he could borrow her Kodak Instamatic, if she still had it. Yes, he could, and it was in the top drawer of the chest in the hall.

Driving over to the Jerome house, he contemplated his project. He thought that even for a total amateur like him the bishop's head was a simple affair, at least from the outside. Broad planes and large roundnesses. No complications of deep furrows, wrinkles, clefts, or awkward ears to deal with.

Last night before going to bed he had taken a fist-size ball of modeling clay and, working more with his visual memory and his fingers than with his eyes, had roughed out a little bishop's head. Not bad. Not bad at all. Add a little more clay on top for the dome of the head, and just a jovial suggestion of a rich underchin . . . Yes.

He went to bed quietly happy.

If the life-size head didn't work out as well, if he botched it, that was Jerome's hard luck. After all, he wasn't paying a penny, and the experience of being sculpted would be a nice ego bath for him.

In any case, his own purpose would be accomplished: good

job or botch-up, he would be able to find himself a place on the Jerome scene as long as Tony was in town.

He hadn't called beforehand, a deliberate omission. He wanted to stretch this afternoon's vigil. If the bishop was still asleep, fine. He then would no doubt take some time to dress, and brush his Roman wreath of hair, and to be sure that in the mirror his countenance was at its rosy, glossy best.

Going through the arch in the adobe wall, he saw Lydia in the shadows of the porch, repainting the front door, the same ghost blue. She had turned at the sound of his car stopping and had given him a look which he read with painful clarity: Oh, it's you and not . . .

Or so he thought. Or was he just stepping squarely, really, into the role Tony had cast him for in front of her, nobody-nothing-nowhere Darrell?

"Is your father napping?" he asked forthrightly. "He's expecting me this afternoon. I'm going to try a portrait bust of him."

"Yes, he told me." Was she smiling in amusement or in welcome? "I'll run up and wake him. There's beer in the refrigerator if you'd like some, to urge on inspiration."

They both fell silent as another car stopped squarely in front of the wall arch, a white Mercedes. Darrell watched Tony get out of it.

"Look," he said swiftly, "can't you say you're having drinks and dinner with me? I mean, will you? He's bad news, watch out for him—terribly *terribly* bad news."

Lydia murmured, "What an awful thing to say, you're almost as bad as he is . . . was, rather, yesterday when you . . ."

Tony came up the path in his leisurely own-the-earth way.

"I was just driving past on my way to—and then I found I couldn't. Just hand Darrell that paintpot and brush, I have more entertaining things in mind for you."

Rage rose in Darrell. "I was just telling her to watch out for you, I told her what bad news you were."

Tony placed a hand on the center of his brother's chest and gave him a firm, punishing shove backward. Darrell hit the wet paint of the door, hit it with the back of his new white fisherman's sweater.

## 11

Lydia did not hand her paintpot and brush to Darrell but placed them on the porch floor in a far corner. Not looking at either of them, she said, "I'll go wake Father," and vanished through the door and up the stairs.

Darrell was astonished by the swift strength with which he took himself in hand, something new in his experience. Brawling on the Jeromes' porch, shouts, the usual ugly words, Tony in any case probably getting the better of it verbally and/or physically—no. There was a job to be done.

He turned, went through the open door and along the hall to the back, to the green and trees and the garden. He left silence behind him. Surprised silence?

Lydia knocked at her father's door. "Darrell's here," she called. There was an answering sleepy rumble. She went into her own room across the hall and in the act of pulling a jade linen sundress out of the closet paused for a second. Was she really going to go off with him? After that little scalding scene on the porch? Even while questioning herself, she was shedding her work shorts and shirt and slipping on the dress, its spaghetti straps bow-tied on the shoulders, dashing cold water in her face and brushing her hair. When you were thirsty, you didn't say no to a brimming beaker of the best and most expensive cold sizzling champagne.

An unnerving thought presented itself to her: perhaps women who considered themselves nice enough, mannerly enough, sensitive enough, didn't actually mind having two males quarreling over them? It hadn't happened to her before, so she had no solid basis for judgment.

Tony wandered into the hall, listening for her. He saw a framed watercolor hanging modestly in a shadowy portion of the hall, a haze of silvery-looking trees, a foreground explosion of sunflowers. Memory tickled.

As Lydia came down the stairs, he said, "Wood nymphs know how to choose their colors," with vivid approval, and, "Speaking of that, where's my watercolor?"

"In my studio, follow me." Her studio was a little, serenely bare room facing north. The watercolor was on her drawing board. He looked at it, nodded, and she said, "I'd want five hundred for it."

She had never asked for and got at the most more than three hundred for a small watercolor. Was she doing this because he probably calculated innate value by price? Or, just possibly, was she doing it for Darrell, a form of financial scolding?

"Okay. I like it. I'll pick it up when we get back." As he started the car, he said, "Before we immediately abandon the crude subject of dollars and cents, do you think Lally might part with that chest in her hall? It's early San Sebastiano, chestnut, a girl I know collects the stuff."

"I don't know, you'd have to ask her. Lally doesn't cherish objects, like furniture. A lot of old things were just left in the house when they bought it. Is it worth a lot?"

"Seven, eight thousand, at least."

Lydia found herself not thinking very clearly in this crackling takeover presence. Fumbling for words, she said, "But Lally might not want to sell bits and pieces of the house out from under . . ."

"Her heir. Darrell." A man of verbal shortcuts, he added, "Which is why I wasn't all that surprised to find he'd left mending nets or painting hulls or whatever he could find in Rockport to do—for fairer fields."

"Your humble subject is ready, my boy," called Jerome through the screen top of the glass hall door. Darrell wagged beckoning fingers and he emerged into the sunlight, fawn linen knickers and a fawn and white striped shirt, face showing the refreshment of a good nap. Leaning heavily on his knobby black walking stick, he made his slow way across the lawn.

"I thought sunlight first, full sunlight, for planes and so on, sharp contrasts, and then outdoor shadow, and then some indoor studies," Darrell said, still amazed at his own clap of cool, his ability to walk away from dangerous rage.

The shooting went pleasantly. The wind had dropped and the air was hot and fragrant with the scent of iris and roses, and in color almost visibly blue. Darrell, knowing that most people were inclined to distrust people who made any project look easy, made it look complicated. Profile, three-quarter, full face, on the right, then the same on the left; taking quite a while squinting into the viewer before clicking the shutter. Then a number of shots from the rear, still in bright sunlight, Jerome seated on a white-painted garden bench.

The subject, who had been silent, said, "No one ever thinks of the *back* of one's head. Does it look all right?" He put a hand to the gray fluffy hair at the nape.

"Quite—oh, well, you've seen those classical busts in museums and libraries and colleges and places," Darrell said. "Now we'll do you in the shade. Diffused light, you know. A whole different aspect to the thing."

What a pleasant kind of feeling, to sound as if he knew what the hell he was talking about.

Speaking of talking about . . .

"You have a nice setup here," he said. "Turn your head just an inch to the left. Privacy, garden, lawn, trees, mountain view, the works, not all that land to take care of, like Lally has."

"Lally? All that land?"

"I'll wait till your eyebrows drop back to where they belong . . . okay now."

Jerome transferred the raise of his eyebrows into the tone of his voice, a little haughty, as though in some way he had been unfavorably compared with Lally Hyde.

"Just four acres, and several she has picked up here and there for possible future sale . . . Why, my friends the Harnetts not half a mile from here have a hundred acres, to say nothing of a swimming pool that circles their rather immense house like a moat. Another friend, Mrs. Wilberforce, has five hundred acres, some of them devoted to the breeding of racehorses. One of her horses, Grandee, won the Belmont Stakes last year."

"Mmmm," Darrell murmured in the half-listening way of the absorbed artist. His chance arrow had hit the black center of the target.

It had occurred to him in a midnight waking that maybe a visit to the County Assessor's Office was not a great idea. Suppose Lally died suddenly. Suppose for some reason her death was looked into. He had a vision of some helpful underling at the Assessor's Office volunteering information to the police.

. . . Well, just a few days (weeks?) back, a young man came in wanting to find out the extent of Mrs. Hyde's property. Yes, I can describe him—very dark eyes, almost black-looking, black hair, thirtyish, and I remember his voice because it was so deep, he sounded like the kind of a voice you hear on the radio . . .

Round it out, thanks to the bishop, at six acres. Two hundred and ten thousand dollars. Not counting the house.

Finishing up with Jerome in tree shade, Darrell said, "Now some indoor shots, if I'm not tiring you out."

"Not at all. But indoor, with this magnificent light?"

"By flash," Darrell explained. "Removes all shadows from the face. A different study of you."

He helped Jerome to his feet and held one arm while Jerome made heavy use of his stick with the other during the hobble to the house.

He sank with a sigh of relief into his recliner. Sounding as if it was an almost-forgotten matter of the idlest interest, he asked, "Did I see Lydia going off with a man in a white Mercedes? Did you meet the chap?"

"Yes. He's my brother." Darrell fitted a flash cube into the Instamatic.

"Married? Not that that means anything these days."

Unclerical thing to say, Darrell thought, but then reminded himself that Jerome was not in Holy Orders.

"Was. Not at the moment. Look straight at me. Chin up a bit more." A colorless flare of light.

"Oh. What's his occupation? He doesn't live somewhere near?"

"He works mostly on the Coast, lives there, he's in the movie business."

"Then what's he doing here? Visiting Lally?"

"Profile, please." Another pop of light. "Filming a few sequences of something or other."

"Not the man I read about in the papers? Tony Hyde? Somehow one hadn't thought—" Jerome cut himself off abruptly.

That I could possibly have a brother of such ringing name and fame, Darrell finished silently, for him.

The bland smoothness of Jerome's face made his expressions that much more readable. Alarm. Greed. Pride. Alarm again?

"Oh well, our young Lydia would hardly expect, or want, to ally herself with . . ."

Darrell was angry at the selfish downgrading of his own

daughter, just to reassure himself that Tony Hyde posed no threat to him whatever.

"Perhaps you haven't noticed that, in her own way . . . how attractive she is. Right profile. Then the back, and that's it."

He was pleased to see the look of dismay flit across Jerome's face. At the door, he said, "I'm going off to collect the beer Lydia offered me earlier. Thanks for being so patient."

After they had left behind the crude subject of dollars and cents, Lydia felt herself somewhat at a loss for easy casual words. He was driving south along Rio Grande Boulevard, faster than she liked to go on this curving road.

How about, "Where are you taking me?" No, that sounded as if she was totally in his hands, in every way.

How about, "Where are you staying?" No, too open to misinterpretation, a direct inquiry about his hotel room.

He broke his own self-contained silence. "I thought, a drink, believe it or not I haven't had one all day. Where's a place where there aren't men wearing Stetsons?"

"Let's see . . . there's a pleasant restaurant called the Chimisa near Old Town, not far from here, with a nice little bar looking into the back garden. Take the next turn to your left." Lovely safe topic. "Do you mean to say you haven't eaten either? I could have . . ."

"Too busy," Tony said.

Was this an invitation to ask him about his work? Show her excitement at being taken out by an internationally known writer-director? Tell him, dwell on, how much she liked his films? She had only seen one of them and most of it she hadn't liked at all, even though she perfectly well understood why it was a smash. There were some scenes where she had to close her eyes.

She couldn't make this plunge into breathless, starry-eyed admiration.

"You do," she said, "cut quite a swathe," and saw from the surprised amusement about his mouth that she had said exactly the right thing. He had been waiting for the ohs and ahs and was pleased, she thought, that he had chosen—for the moment—a girl who felt free to bypass the obvious.

There were only five other people in the ferny little bar at the Chimisa and they spent a good deal of their time gazing raptly at Tony, sitting at a window table across from Lydia, his extraordinary face and head seen against an outer blaze of yellow coreopsis. Lydia was taken aback to feel in herself an unfounded glow of ego: reflected glory.

She said she'd have a scotch and water (knowing that he had probably expected some provincial female choice, such as a frozen daiquiri) and he ordered a dry martini for himself. "Ridiculous hour to drink a martini," he said, "but I'm having to shove everything forward. I have to be up at four in the morning, sunrise scene on the Sandias. Keep your fingers crossed for me—I don't want the cameras to have to cope with more than one goddamned jet trail across my fifteenth-century English skies."

He didn't, self-effacingly, murmur, but talked in normal pitch and was of course listened to; Lydia gathered that for him the other people in the bar did not count, were not there.

He asked her about her work, and listened with apparent intent interest to her brief summary of it.

"Why don't you just paint, instead of trying to teach a mixed bag of no doubt louts? You're good."

She smiled. "Have you ever heard of such a thing as money matters? Oh yes, we started our conversation with money."

"If you were nearer at hand, I could be your patron," he said thoughtfully. Their drinks arrived and without any request for a menu he said to the waitress, "Bring me two broiled lamb chops, medium, and a lot of sliced tomatoes, put a little oil and basil on them, like a good girl." She departed pink and happy for the kitchen and Tony saluted Lydia with his glass and then devoted himself swiftly to its contents.

Time passed with amazing speed. She nursed her long drink and he ate his food and then ordered Mexican beer. After a second bottle, he looked at his watch.

"Yes, time enough," he said. "Let's go to my hotel and get ourselves acquainted. In person."

Lydia had been half expecting something more or less along these lines. She was not naïve. A nice little romp with a girl I met, terrific eyes—terrific for Albuquerque, that is . . . But the gentlemanly naturalness of his manner, the clear assumption behind it, surprised her a little.

She leisurely finished the last half inch of her drink. "I haven't glamorous film deadlines like you but I do have some of my own. Father's Sunday dinner. Somewhat of a holy ritual. Always at six on the dot. We must deliver me back right now so I can get the roast in the oven."

He looked for a moment puzzled, perhaps wondering if she was playing some out-of-style game. Oh no, my dear sir, I'm not *quite* that easy. But keep trying.

"All right, then, until the next time," he said. "I don't think we could really improve our relationship right under your father's nose."

Fifteen minutes later he dropped her at the arch in the adobe wall. Lydia, going up the path, saw Darrell sitting on the top step of the porch, drinking a can of beer.

"Welcome home," he said. "That was a quickie."

The moment the words were out he could have kicked himself. What had he meant by that? Why had he said it?

Lydia, who had imperturbably retained her color during Tony's invitation to join him in his bed, blushed, mainly with anger.

She walked up the steps past him and closed the front door behind her with a firmness just short of a slam.

Tense with embarrassment, Darrell arrived at the Jeromes'
front porch at precisely twenty-eight minutes after eight.
The door was wide open. Lydia came out, a morning scent
and freshness about her, wearing for her teaching duties a
paisley-printed jersey pants suit.

Darrell got some awkward words out. "I've been worrying
since I last saw you, about . . . I mean, I didn't mean . . ."

*That was a quickie*, their meeting glances repeated to each
other.

"For God's sake, Darrell, what on earth does it matter what
you meant? Happy greenhouse to you." But she didn't walk
down the porch steps, she ran down them.

From the living room a voice called, "Is that Henry Moore
I hear? Or would Sir Jacob Epstein be more to the point?
Come and greet your subject."

And as Darrell came in to say hello, "Are you getting too
much sun too soon, my boy? You're quite a powerful color."

Darrell wondered at what age he would cease to blush. Or
was his color the sting of a slap across the face?

"And how is dear Lally?" Jerome was heartily attacking a
plate of scrambled eggs and bacon and had already done a
neat job on half a cantaloupe.

"Fine. Busy. Cleaning out a pile of old files."

"Files?" Jerome paused for a sip of coffee. "I had never
somehow pictured Lally as a woman who filed anything."

"No, Tom's files, from his office. They were dumped on
her when the business closed down. They're cluttering up

the apartment over the garage and we're thinking of . . . or rather, she thinks she might rent it."

"Good idea. A fire hazard in any case, masses of old papers." He blinked suddenly, his cup held motionless several inches above his saucer. Darrell took the little silence as an opportunity to remove himself and get to work on the greenhouse.

Lally was on her way from the front door to the garage when, through the open driveway gate, the dog ran in.

It stopped a few feet from her, its long plumy tail moving just a little, back and forth, doubtful hopeful tail.

It—and Lally now changed the pronoun to she—might be a Samoyed, or a spitz, or even a Great Pyrenees. She was no expert on breeds; her own predilections had always run to Airedales, of which in her past there were three. This looked to be a young dog, with a sumptuous white coat gleaming in the sunlight. Her eyes were dark and deep, large, and thickly lashed in white, her muzzle broad. She was obviously thirsty, pink tongue hanging out.

"Go home," Lally said in a kind firm voice. "Go home, girl."

The dog stood just as firmly still, her tail motion picking up momentum.

"You're valuable, whoever you are," Lally further addressed her. "You just can't go around idly visiting, and Andalusia Trail is a terrible risk for loose dogs." She noticed that the dog had no collar bearing an identifying tag, but that wasn't unusual here. She cast her memory north and south along the road and could remember no such dog in anybody's yard. She would certainly have registered the animal if she had seen it; a beautiful thing.

"Oh well, we'll give you some water and then ask you politely to go home again." Dogs off the leash were sometimes frightening, hostile, but this one wasn't. She trotted close at

Lally's heels into the kitchen and drank a little of the water in the bowl Lally put down and then backed away from it, shivering a little. Fright? Longing to be back where she belonged?

"Now then." Out to the front yard, the two of them. "*Go home!*"

In response, the dog walked past her and lay down on the wide stone doorstep, gentle eyes pleading, silky white lashes flickering.

"Oh hell. Well, you can stay here a little while, until . . ." Until what? She hadn't the heart to shoo the dog into the curving dangerous narrow road. She closed the gate and went in to call the Animal Humane Association. Not, never, Animal Rescue. They would take that elegant creature to a pound. She was obviously not first and foremost an attack or guard dog and with her size would be an expense to feed. If she wasn't adopted within a set number of days, then . . .

A nice young woman took the call. "I'm reporting a lost dog which ran into my yard. White, young, female, could be a Samoyed or a spitz, but I'm not all that sure of my breeds."

"Does she hold her tail up or down? How high does she stand?"

"Tail down, but that might be fear, or distress. About two and a half feet high and I'd say twenty-four inches or so from neck to where the tail starts."

Her name, address, and telephone number were taken down. "We've had no report on anything that sounds like this dog yet, but you say she's only just turned up at your house. You'll keep her there in the meantime? And keep an eye on the classified ads."

Lally went and got the water bowl to place near the dog. The sun had been very hot on the front step and now she lay on a bed of cool green Parma violets against the base of the house wall, under one of the window boxes planted with sweet peas. "Off my violets!" In answer, the dog rolled over on her back, paws dangling: a gesture of complete trust.

"Well, now you have a name, I can't keep calling you *you*. Your name is Parma." She patted the dog's stomach and then headed for the garage, the stairs, and the files.

Her method of clearing them out, with the goal of either selling the metal cases or having them carted to the city dump, was to glance at great speed through each large handful of paper. When, here and there, she caught sight of anything involving a very large sum of money, or any locally well-known name (such as former Mayor Cortez, who had been a client of Tom's), she placed the paper in a manila folder on which she had written "Hold."

If the folder or additional folders got too fat they could be put in a carton and shoved out of sight under the bed in the guest room, at present Darrell's.

After forty-five minutes of this her head was aching. The heat under the flat garage roof was intense. How had Bill ever stood it? But then, he'd stayed here only during the college year, not in summers. It would have to be insulated, the roof, when they had gotten things in shape to rent the apartment. To poor Joan and her boys.

Don't soften and sag about that, Lally exhorted herself. Don't let up on what was now the main and perhaps last large goal of her life: repairing Darrell's future. Two days or so of work assembling a greenhouse hardly constituted a budding career.

She was in the J-to-M file when her scooping hand pulled out a thick folder marked "Jerome." No prying, now. She knew Lydia's income, on which she'd pay the usual taxes. She probably was able to take her father as a dependent, although he did have a tiny annual income from an aunt's estate. Enough, Lydia had told her once, to pay for his knicker suits and most of his brandy.

In any case, none of her business. The triplicate forms

could safely be tossed away. The bishop was a devoted custodian of family papers and documents; in fact, his personal collection and examination of the daily mail was a ritual never to be interfered with. "It gets him out rain, shine, or snow," Lydia said. "It's good for him, I suppose." "And," tartly from Lally, "do you suppose he steams open your letters?" After short consideration, "I don't think so. It just helps to remind him that he's head of the house."

Yes, throw the Jerome file away. But one quick look, in case there would be a will there, or something else of vital importance.

There was a carbon of a letter to the bishop from Tom; the date caught her eye because it had been written just six months before Tom died. She scanned the letter. Then she read it.

"Dear Mr. Jerome: I can understand your desire for secrecy in the matter, or at least your aunt's wish that you should benefit from this discreet handling of funds. I do wonder if you're wise in keeping your good fortune from Lydia. However, in the matter of confidences between mothers and daughters—however separated by distance and circumstances —I am anything but an expert.

"Your aunt's lawyers will no doubt have advised you of the following but I do want to underline its importance. Obtain Lydia's full signature in any way you think decent and proper. This can then be appended (taped) by your lawyers to a power of attorney which would enable Lydia legally to claim the funds in the event of your death. Again, I am probably repeating myself on matters already taken care of, but if you determine to continue silent on the subject, write a letter to Lydia to be opened on your death, informing her that she is your heir and has power of attorney over an account in Switzerland. This letter goes to Sellers and Penderby, to be held by them and sent to her at the time of your death.

"By the way, you may rest assured that this is a very highly respected law firm, one of the finest in San Francisco, and you may rely on them totally. However, as you requested, I have as an invisible second party to the information memorized the Swiss account number.

"I hope your health will soon show signs of improvement. Yours truly, Thomas Hyde."

Lally had been sitting to her back-aching work on an old vinyl-covered hassock. Very slowly and neatly, she folded the sheet of paper in four and put it in her pants pocket.

She got up and went down the stairs and across the yard. Parma rose from her leafy bed to greet her, a patch of sunlight striking crystal in the snow of the waving tail, eyes softly beautiful, welcoming. From nowhere came a thought, how simple and innocent a dog can be, how vile in behavior a man can be. But she was still too stunned for contact with anything or anybody.

She went into the kitchen, reheated the morning coffee, and sugared a steaming mug of it. Now, she ordered herself, sit down and think this out. Including what if anything you are going to do about it.

People, as far as she knew, didn't put five hundred or two thousand dollars in numbered Swiss bank accounts. Her sketchy, layman's comprehension of the matter suggested strongly to her that you put large sums of money into these accounts, for purposes some of which were no doubt nefarious. The whole point was secrecy.

Secrecy from Lydia. Her father, ill and dependent. A powerful and sometimes painful chain.

Where had the funds come from? Wait a minute. Your aunt's lawyers. San Francisco. Lally remembered years back the bishop going on in a complacent understated way about his Aunt Amelia, who had a very large estate in Marin County (photographs of it, four pages of them, had appeared that month in *House and Garden)* as well as a permanent suite at the Plaza in New York and the same arrangement at the Ritz in Paris.

That was, as far as Lally knew, the only source of great wealth in the Jerome family. She had at the time conceived an idea that the bishop had high hopes in that direction, financially.

But when the aunt had died, five or six years ago, she had left Percival Jerome what Lydia said amounted to an annual clothes allowance, fifteen hundred dollars or so.

"Your aunt's wish that you should benefit from this discreet handling of funds . . ." From her own past came a memory of an Uncle William who, in order to bypass death duties, had in the decade before he died handed over comfortable pre-burial monies and land to his sons and daughters as outright gifts. Was that what Aunt Amelia had done? Lally remembered reading about her death in the Sunday New York *Times*. Her husband, who had predeceased her, was a Texan: oil. She was reported to have left a private fortune in excess of six million dollars. When in time she heard about the bishop's clothing allowance, it had struck Lally that even for a lazy demanding incubus like Percy, it was a dirty, a very dirty, trick.

But why, when he could presumably live in splendor, cosseted and waited upon around the clock—when he could take his obscure physical problems to the Mayo Clinic, or to European spas—why the secrecy steadily maintained?

The annual interest on a thumping sum of money would certainly have made a significant difference in the Jerome household. Unless, as she herself did with her money market account in her local bank, he had arranged to have the interest automatically reinvested.

She had a deep certainty that Lydia knew nothing of any of this. Lydia had an openness, an honesty, almost a transparency, which Lally found one of her most endearing qualities.

She reached into her pocket and took out the carbon of the letter again. "However, in the matter of confidences between mothers and daughters . . ."

Lydia was, she knew, on amiable if physically remote terms with her mother. "After all," she had once said, "she didn't leave me, I was almost twenty, grown up, and would have been off myself soon, I had no intention of spending my life in Albuquerque. It was my father she left." Unspoken, the hovering following words, but Lally sensed them: And I don't know that I entirely blame her for that.

Mother and daughter wrote each other three or four times a year and exchanged Christmas presents.

Had the bishop feared that, hearing of his windfall, his ex-wife might come running back to him? A woman who could dump one man perfectly capable of dumping a second, and making a strategic return to the scene? That could be one reason for his silence on the subject.

The other, which emerged as quite real, dark, and ugly, was that it assured the caretaker role in which Lydia was locked, ensured it indefinitely, until the day of his death.

The bishop was now sixty-seven years old. Lally had ascertained this once, feeling what she told herself was a most uncharitable interest, on Lydia's behalf, in when he might reasonably be expected to be gathered to his ancestors.

He could live another fifteen years. Or longer.

Why hadn't Tom, her own dear Tom, told her about the matter? The answer was all too clear: she would have fumed over it, burst with it, and let the truth out with a crash.

Which brought her full circle to what she was going to do about it now.

Walk right into it, face him with it, loud and clear? Destroy him? Perhaps *them*? What would it do to Lydia?

No. Strike some sort of private bargain with him, just between the two of them. Demand that he make up some sort of plausible story for Lydia. This should present no great difficulty to an accomplished liar.

Tell her that his aunt's will had specified that if heir A or heir B died the money was to revert to him, lots and lots of money. And that he had been informed by the San Francisco law firm of Sellers and Penderby that A or B had met an unfortunate early end.

He hadn't, the bishop would go on, told her before because he didn't want to raise false hopes for either of them.

Yes. To remind herself of this solution to the problem, she turned the letter over and penciled a few notes on the back of it.

But not right now, not today. All this thinking about death, the bishop's eventually, and the imaginary heir, had had a tiring and draining effect on her.

She would soon be seventy-four herself; hardly a tower of strength. And it might be a windmill she was tilting at, not a windfall. There was no proof that this Swiss hoard was large. It might only be, say, fifty thousand dollars.

Relatively modest as she had always felt her own circumstances to be, she would be worth a good deal more than that, to young Darrell, upon her demise.

No, put the whole thing aside for at least today. Sleep on it.

". . . to sleep, perchance to dream . . . the undiscovered country from whose bourn no traveler returns . . ."

"*No!*" cried Lally out loud, to encircling death.

## 13

Lydia got home at close to five o'clock. She was tired and hot after taking, in the school van, a party of ten of her art students—one and all depressingly talentless—to the forested east side of the Sandia range for several hours of sketching in pastel.

After the school year ended in mid-May, Miss Withington's turned itself into a Summer Learning Camp. Art, music, and show riding were offered, as well as discreet special tutoring for girls lagging behind in subjects at their own private schools.

It had occurred to Lydia, as it did at least once a week, that she was not the stuff of which teachers are made, or should be.

Oh well, a living. One oughtn't to allow oneself this occasional feeling of wandering around without point or purpose in a gray timeless nowhere.

There was a sound of hammering near the back door, Darrell at work on his greenhouse. She expected at any moment a protest from her napping father, to which she would have to answer that you cannot *whisper* a structure of metal, wood, and plastic together; but when she went upstairs to shower and change, his bedroom door was still closed. Perhaps he found the noises of somebody else's hard labor a form of lullaby.

When she came down again, fresh in a cool white float of a dress, Darrell was in the kitchen, opening and closing the doors of wall cabinets in an indecisive way. "I'm looking for a mug, or a glass," he explained. "Hello, Lydia. Ice water is what I'm after." He presented a picture common to those working at a temperature of over a hundred degrees in the sun: soaked to the skin, including eyelashes and hair.

Lydia found him an outsize yellow mug and got out ice cubes. She filled the cup with cold tap water, shook the ice cubes around in it, and watched while he rinsed his now Indian-red face at the sink, and his hands. He reached for paper toweling and dried himself off.

He had been bracing himself most of his working day for this moment. You have to, he had kept saying mentally, start *somewhere*.

As she handed him the yellow mug, he bent forward and very lightly kissed her temple close to the hairline. She smelled delightful, freesias or something. "By way of good afternoon, Lydia," he said in a voice which had been meant to come out soft and easy and was closer to a croak.

From the doorway into the hall, a voice said, "Is this the way they make love in Albuquerque?"

Tony. Splendid in a white linen shirt and shorts, the belt for the shorts provided by an expensive silk foulard tie. There was someone behind him, a girl, in the shadows of the hall.

"The door was open," he said. "I knocked on the jamb but you must have been running water. I've come around to collect my picture."

Lydia went out into the hall, Darrell close behind her.

"This is Sid Sims, by the way," Tony said. "Lydia—" Then he stopped, obviously having forgotten her last name. "And my brother Darrell."

Well, who else? Tony's top star, Sid for the never-used Sidonie, late twenties, bony memorable face, sweat-soaked mass of dun-blond hair half over her face, dirty chinos and either Tony's violet shirt from yesterday or its twin, bare feet.

In half-apology, she said, "He sits on cool rocks in deep

shade and tells other people what to do. Me, I work. Tony, do you think your brother's . . . girl could produce something wet that isn't water?"

Lydia felt Tony's eyes on her, piercingly examining. She had a feeling that, ridiculous as it was, he was in the act of putting her back in her place in some invisible corner from which he had reached a generous hand to pull her briefly out. Would you like to see the kind of woman I really get on with, Lydia Something, and who really gets on with me?

"We haven't time to slake you, Sid," he said. "We're due down the road. About the picture . . . ?"

Lydia left the little group in the hall, went into her studio, and brought out with some remote inkling of distress her watercolor.

"I don't know if you want to attend to matting and glassing and framing and all that or if—"

"Wait a minute," he interrupted. "It might be for Sid. Do you like it, Sid?"

The girl took the sheet of paper, held it at arm's length, pushed wet hair back from over her eyes with the other hand, and then said, "No."

The naked rudeness seemed somehow natural to her, nothing vicious behind it, or nasty, just honest reaction unrepressed by any clutter of good manners.

Lydia reached out and all but snatched the watercolor from the thin brown hand. Tony at the same time made a grab for the other edge of it, and accidentally or purposefully gave his wrist a sharp twist. The watercolor was the loser in this tug-of-war. Tough as the paper was, it tore with a crisp snapping sound, tore roughly in half.

Out of the corner of one eye, Lydia was aware of the back door opening and closing, Darrell running away from unpleasantness, from conflict, from his brother.

She felt an inward shaking herself and hoped it didn't show on the outside. The back door opened again and Darrell went past her, closed the front door and stood against it. She saw, appalled, that he had a hammer in his hand.

"How much were you going to pay for it, Tony?" he asked. Tony for the first time seemed to become aware of the presence at the door. And the claw hammer.

"Five hundred," he said. "Drop that hammer. Are you crazy?"

"If I say so myself, I have dead aim when I put my talents to it." Darrell swung the hammer gently at his side. "Right at your face. If you haven't got that much cash on you, your friend can probably lend you the rest."

"For God's sake, Darrell, *no,*" Lydia managed.

"Keep out of it, dear," the word coming easily to him. "As Tony said, families sometimes talk very frankly to each other."

Tony laughed, a high hard laugh, and Darrell could almost smell the very real fear coming from him, his beautiful head, his priceless face, at the mercy of a flung claw hammer.

"I can deal with the sane but not with the round-the-bend," he said to Sid. "I have about two seventy-five. What have you got?"

With her eyes fixed on the hand, the hammer, Sid dug into the leather bag hung by a strap over her shoulder. She passed him her wallet and he took out four fifty-dollar bills, a twenty, and five ones.

Counting them out aloud, he dropped bill after bill on the floor. "Okay, Darrell. I could take you both to court but it wouldn't in any way be worth it. The names would hardly pay off—an aspiring local art teacher and an obscure layabout brother."

Darrell turned the knob behind him with his free hand and held the door open. "Have a nice time," he said, "down the road."

He waited, holding his homely weapon, until he heard the sound of a car outside the wall starting up.

THE GIFT HORSE                    99

Over head-ringing shock, Lydia murmured, "David and Goliath. Only he turned out not to be so much of a Goliath after all. And I must say you were rather a scary David . . . Would you really have thrown that hammer? Of course, I won't have anything to do with"—the toe of her sandal touched the corner of one of the fifty-dollar bills—"any of this."

"No, I wouldn't have, but he couldn't know that. And you will take the money, because to get it for you I've drawn a nice picture of myself as a dangerous madman."

"No," she said, "no, you haven't . . ." her shock still affecting the sound of her voice. Making it shaky, and breathless. And uncertain.

From the top of the stairs, a voice called, "What's all that money doing all over the floor?" Jerome stood in the upper hall, in a polka-dotted silk robe.

"Lydia sold a painting." Darrell bent, gathered up the bills, and, folding them, tucked them into the pocket of Lydia's white dress. "And now I'm going to have that drink of water I never managed to get around to and go back to work."

After a short time he found himself hollow and exhausted, and not just with sun and sweat and labor. Better knock off, before Jerome came hobbling out for inspection and conversation. It suddenly occurred to him that what had happened in the hall had probably put an end to any need for his off-hours guard duties at the Jerome house. But since yesterday his fingers had been itching to get at it, get started, on the life-size head of the bishop.

The white dog came to greet him when he opened Lally's front door. Her eyes were inquiring but not hostile. Darrell, thinking that Lally might be minding the dog for a friend, gave the heavy silky coat an absentminded pat. "Hello there, whoever you are."

Hearing him, Lally came out of the kitchen. "I'll explain her later," she said. "Someone called this afternoon wanting to talk to you, a young woman, station KUNM. I have the number here."

He called and got the same girl with the kind manner he had talked to on Friday morning. She said that a friend of hers had been promoted to assistant program director of station KRCW and had a lot of ideas about beefing up the programming.

"I was really very much struck by your voice even though, as I said, we use only volunteers, and I told him about you. Sort of, I said, Cyril Ritchard, but deeper, organ-music tone. He's interested. You have no idea how hard it is to find super voices. You might give him a call, wait, I have the number somewhere—oh, right here. His name is Don Duff."

Darrell called the station and was predictably enough put on hold for Don Duff. He waited four endless minutes, and was about to hang up and try later when, with Lally listening anxiously in the doorway, the man came on, ending a sentence to someone else, ". . . and for God's sake be sure the coffee's hot this time." Darrell identified himself and Don Duff said, "Mmmm, yes, you're new here? You haven't worked for any other station here?"

Darrell forbore to say he hadn't worked for any other station anywhere.

"Pick up anything handy, a book, a paper, read me a paragraph, will you?"

The evening paper, the *Tribune*, lay over the arm of the chair he was sitting in. Darrell picked it up and read, at random, from the Letters to the Editor column:

"I feel it is high time that someone complained publicly about the chairs in the departure and arrival lounges at Albuquerque International Airport. They are the ugliest, most awkward, most uncomfortable chairs I have ever sat or tried to sit on, they are simply not constructed for the human frame. There is nothing remotely resembling these mon-strosities in any other airport in this country in my experi-ence, and I mean from Savannah to San Diego, my work involves a good deal of air travel. Surely those comfortable plastic scoop chairs are not beyond the budget of our fair city's increasingly busy air terminal?"

Darrell only stumbled once, toward the end. Duff burst out laughing. "Those god-awful chairs, yes. Well said—particu-larly by you. Great, terrific, I mean really good sound. I don't suppose you have two heads? Not that that would matter on radio. On the other hand, of course, I'm not promising any-thing." There was a gulping sound; apparently the coffee was hot enough.

"Tell you what," Duff continued. "This place is a mad-house and appointments go down the drain. I can spot a little oasis later in the week. I'll give you a ring from my house and you might drop around for a drink and a bit of taping. You're not, by the way, a dedicated drinker? As you know, there's a lot of that seeping hither and thither in this business."

"An occasional glass of this or that," Darrell assured him.

"Okay. Stand by. Don't talk to anyone else until I get first chop."

Replacing the receiver, Darrell turned a slightly bemused face to Lally. "He sounds interested."

"Tell me what he said."

While he was telling her, he was thinking how odd it all was. He had come out here empty and blank and now . . .

Hardly able to wait until he got his hands on his block of clay. And Lydia . . . And an approaching appointment that might mean work and money . . .

"Maybe after all I won't even have to think any more about . . ." He was horrified to realize he was saying this out loud.

"Think about what?"

About the possible purposes to which nylon cord, or a Browning shotgun, or a wicked-headed hoe could be put.

"About maybe having to shove off to San Francisco to try to pry some work out of Adam."

## 14

Darrell's unexpected swift grasp at opportunity surprised and pleased Lally. She had been fully prepared for something like "Oh, good, I'll give her a call later in the week when I finish this job up."

If he can jump into things, she thought, what am I hanging back for, putting off until tomorrow something I don't yet want to face?

It also occurred to her, as she opened the oven door to stir her baked beef stew, that the interview with the bishop could not be conducted with anyone else on the scene or near it. There might be some awful commotion, shouting, God knows what. Lydia must be safely at her school and Darrell safely elsewhere. Just the two of them to talk, she and Percy. No one to overhear them but the grackles and finches in the trees.

But set it up anyway. Give him time to think, to digest it. Do it by telephone. Try to do it this evening.

She didn't exactly admit to herself that in any case, in a matter of this delicacy, it would be safer that way, for her.

At dinner, she asked Darrell when he thought he'd be finished with the greenhouse.

Having begun on his stew with immense appetite, he swallowed a chunk of very hot potato with a grimace of pain, cooled his throat with beer, and said, "Probably end of the day tomorrow, Wednesday noon at the latest, but he says he may want extra stuff done then, a center table and things."

"Yes, well, but the main job will be finished and you may by then have heard from your radio man."

The scent of the stew and the sound of the voices at the kitchen table drifted out to Parma, asleep on her side in the near walled garden. Lally had already given her a meal of beef trimmings, cooked carrots, and torn-up bread and butter, but now she came to the back door and leaped against the screening, with a pleading half-bark, half-cry.

"Shall I let her in?"

"No, I don't want to get too used to her and vice versa, it's unkind to the dog."

Looking at her through the screen, Darrell said, "She's a beauty. Reminds you in some strange way of the unicorn in the garden. Why don't you just keep her?"

"I could literally be accused of highway robbery if the owner drove by and spotted her. She's valuable, you can see that. There'll probably be an ad in the morning classified section. And anyway"—suddenly feeling and looking unaccountably weary—"you're enough to take on for the moment, young Darrell."

He grinned happily at her. "You must admit things are looking up. A few inches up, at least."

Unused to secrecy herself, Lally had a little trouble with her telephone arrangements. The Jeromes' dinner would be eaten and the dishes done by eight-thirty, and Lydia was not the type to listen on extensions. Darrell, tired, was reading in the living room, really reading now *The Proud Tower.* Should she send him on an errand? What errand? She disliked retreating to the phone in Tom's office and closing the door; if Darrell came into the kitchen for something to eat or drink with his book, he would wonder at it, perhaps—heavens, no! —listen outside the closed door from sheer curiosity.

"I hate to trouble you, dear, but could you take the car and go to M and R Liquors on Fourth Street, I keep forgetting that I'm supposed to have a glass of port wine before I go to

bed, a touch of anemia, nothing serious but the doctor said
. . ."

Darrell off, she sat in the armchair by the telephone and
called the Jerome house. The bishop, she knew, usually went
to bed or, in his term, retired about ten-thirty. To his "Hello"
she said, "Lally. Is Lydia around?"

"No, she was invited to a gallery affair, an opening."

"You might close your door anyway, in case she's fed up
with the show in no time flat."

"Close my *door—!*"

"This is a very private conversation, just between you and
me," Lally pressed on unwillingly.

There was an odd grunting sound, then a pause, then
Percy's voice again. "Something to do with that nephew of
yours, that film man, and Lydia, perhaps?"

"No. Something to do with a letter I found from Tom to
you in Tom's files, about a numbered Swiss bank account."
The silence at the other end was a little frightening and to fill
it in Lally rushed ahead. "I assume you haven't spent all your
aunt's money, or maybe none of it. Your establishment gives
no sign of being run in Rolls-Royce style." In spite of herself,
anger caught her up. "No Paris or New York or anywhere for
Lydia, just that blasted school, and be sure you're home on
time to fix something dainty for Father's dinner—"

"First of all, I think you've gone mad," he said in a trembling voice. "Second, is this some kind of attempt at blackmail? Third, I have no idea what you're talking about."

"I haven't time for long explanations—or to read you this
letter from Tom, the carbon of it rather. I want to assure you
of one thing, to calm you down. Calm both of us down. No
one, *no* one, will know about this from me. But I do want to
have a short session with you when you're alone, when the
house is empty, to discuss matters."

"There are no matters to discuss." The trembling made
this a fluttering near-whisper.

"I have an idea which will set things straight right away and will cause you absolutely no embarrassment. I won't go into it now. I'm sure that one way or another this has been a shock to you and I wanted to give you plenty of time to get your breath back. And no, blackmail doesn't enter into it at all. This is purely disinterested on my part, except for Lydia's place in the picture. The date of the letter by the way is April 3, 1978. Perhaps you have a copy of it in your own files. It might refresh your memory so that when we meet we'll both know exactly what we're talking about. And now, Percy, good night."

Was it just sheer relief that it was over that was causing her to tremble too?

She sat motionless, waiting for her pounding heart to resume its normal rhythm. After a short time, she saw the car headlights at the gate, saw Darrell get out, drive in, and close the gate again. Good boy, he'd remembered about not letting Parma run out into the road. Not that she showed any desire to do so. As he approached the front door, she got up from her place on the step where her head and shoulders had closely hugged the door as she lay there. "Nice girl," she heard Darrell say. "I think I'm going to miss you."

The touch of anemia, and the nightly glass of port, had belonged to a few years back, but she thought a glass right now wouldn't come amiss at all.

There were four advertisements for missing dogs in the Tuesday morning Albuquerque *Journal* but none of them was for a white spitz or Samoyed.

Odd, Lally thought. People had a cruel way of dumping unwanted dogs and cats far from home, in cold half-hopes that somebody might take pity and adopt them. But Parma didn't look like anybody's castoff. Maybe her owner was out of town and didn't know she had wandered away? She picked up the telephone and placed her own classified ad, with orders that it be run in the morning and evening editions for the next two days. Hearing a single crisp bark outside the front door, she went to look out. Parma was with interest and awareness regarding the approach of the man coming to read the gas meter at the left-hand corner of the house.

Lally went out to say hello to him and to be sure Parma didn't go out through the open gate. Parma leaped to greet her with the warmest enthusiasm and affection. "Down, Parma! Good morning, Al."

"Good morning. New dog? Beauty."

"No, lost, I'm trying to find her owner. Anyone in the houses you read meters at lose her, do you know? And what exactly is she?"

"Oh, a spitz," said Al with admiring certainty. "And a very good spitz at that. Young, I'd say. No, I don't connect her with any of my meters. But I'll keep my ears open the rest of my route."

Going about her Tuesday chores, stripping the beds of their sheets and making them up with fresh ones, bundling the laundry into the washing machine in a corner of the kitchen, putting the breakfast dishes away, Lally found herself mentally dwelling on the present state of the bishop, in mixed satisfaction and apprehension.

Would he be lumbering around the living room, unable to sit still in his reclining chair, slashing the air with his heavy stick? She seemed to see his face plum purple, and to hear him swearing out loud, and addressing dreadful statements or even threats to her. No—not with Darrell outside, not with the windows open.

She had only once been an observer of his temper, which she gathered was generally under control but when it erupted alarming. It was a Sunday afternoon, and Lydia while filling his water glass had knocked over a tumbler half full of the last of his brandy. And of course another bottle could not be bought on a Sunday.

Lydia, looking a little pale as the tumbler hit the floor, backed away from the thunderstorm of visible and vocal rage. Lally, having tea in the chair she usually sat in, by the window looking out over the bed of delphinium and baby's breath, got up and began, "See here—" and was savagely told in no uncertain words to remove herself. "I've suddenly got this blinding headache," shouted the bishop. "I want silence, and peace, and a pill, and my own company—*however thirsty it is*—if no one minds."

Well, he was stuck there, no matter how he felt about her this morning, with nothing to do but wait for her visit, which he must be contemplating with horror.

Or was he stuck there? Three or four times a year, Lydia insisted that he take the car out for half an hour. "You never know if *I'd* be flat out, flu or grippe or something, and you've got to for your own sake keep a little in touch with driving." There was a great business of adjusting the seat backward and placing an electric heating pad to comfort the bishop's spine as he took the car at twenty-five miles an hour up and down Rio Grande Boulevard, Lydia at his side treated to every complaint he could find to utter.

But where could he drive to? He couldn't dare run away without hearing her out, hearing her proposition which would cause him "absolutely no embarrassment." If he chose to disappear for a bit, he could have no idea what her reaction, or explosion, or exposure, might be. To Lydia.

In a flash of light accompanied by chill, she thought, He could hardly drive over here in broad daylight, to my house, and—

At night, Darrell was usually home. If and when he was out, there were the locks and chains. But, silly idea, tired old-womanish idea. Picturing an invalid as an attacking brute.

To empty her mind of these visions, she made up a batch of coconut-molasses cookies, put them in the oven to bake, and smiled at Parma's pathetic pleas outside the kitchen door as the oven fragrance reached her nostrils. For the time being, a dog, a big dog, was a comfort to have around. Maybe no one would ever claim Parma. Maybe she would be glad if no one ever did.

With a kickback of conscience, she went to the telephone and called the Animal Humane Association.

She got a different voice this time, high, harassed, but kindly.

"Mrs. Hyde, did you say? Oh, yes, here you are right on my calling list, two names down. Now, let me look at my notes . . . you have a stray Samoyed or spitz, white, young . . ."

"Spitz, it turns out," Lally said.

"Well, a call came in just at closing time yesterday. After checking the files I tried your number but . . ."

"I must have been out picking lettuce for my supper salad," Lally put in a little guiltily.

"The call was from a Mrs. Andrew—"

"Wait till I get a paper and pencil."

"A Mrs. Andrew Cove, 614 Mott Road, telephone number 555-1666. Her spitz ran off—or she thinks it might have been stolen—two days ago. She'd been hoping and praying it would find its way home—her, that is, a female—but finally gave up and called us. Very upset, crying." The Humane Association volunteer felt it an unnecessary note to add that the woman had sounded a little . . . inebriated. "Has your stray been reclaimed by its owner?"

"No. What's the process? Do you call her, or shall I?"

"We would, but . . . with this jam-up, even a lost horse this morning, it would be a help if you did. There might be certain special physical characteristics you've spotted that would help with identification. Find out the dog's name and call her by it and see if she responds."

She dialed Mrs. Cove's number. No answer. It was close to twelve o'clock, the woman could be out shopping, out doing anything. Lally had a sad vision of her driving up this road and down that, stopping to inquire along the way, Have you by any chance seen my spitz?

Nothing to do but shove the vision away, wait a while, try the number in an hour or so.

Mott Road was about a mile east of here, toward the mountains. A mile would be no great distance for a large dog in prime condition to cover on foot. Or maybe someone had indeed tried to steal her, maybe put her in the back of a pickup truck from which she had jumped out at some point.

An hour later, there was still no answer to her call.

Lally ate a late sandwich of cream cheese and sliced tomatoes. It was hard to get down, her stomach in knots, between the bishop and the dog and the weeping woman.

She worked for a while in the round garden while Parma lay on the grass elegantly reflected in the long oval mirror on the door. Finding aphids on the undersides of the geranium leaves, Lally gave them a dose of cold water from the hose. Two or three more cold-water attacks would get rid of them.

The telephone rang and she half ran to answer it. It stopped ringing just as she reached out her hand.

Try the Humane Association again. Had Mrs. Cove called about her spitz? No, she hadn't. Try Mrs. Cove again.

She got a busy signal.

Two minutes later, the line was still busy. This is ridiculous, Lally thought, her nervous system twanging. Her favorite little fruit and vegetable store was on Mott Road. A big bowl of fresh fruit would be nice to have around, good for Darrell. And perhaps strawberry shortcake for dinner.

Take Parma along for the ride. Stop at number 614 and go to the door and plainly and simply say, Is this your dog that I've got here in my car?

Action, she told herself, will be a great relief after you have been spending the day with your mind so far. She called Rose Martinez next door and asked if she could borrow her old Volkswagen for an hour or so; without being close friends, the two women were on easy neighborly terms. Yes, sure she could, just come and get it out of the garage, Rose would run out now with the keys.

Stopping at her own gate, she had no trouble in urging Parma to join her on the front seat. The afternoon was hot and very still, the sky an ugly yellowed oyster glare, oppressively low.

She'd get her main errand over first and then buy her fruit and whipping cream.

Number 614, proclaimed the mailbox in large paste-on numerals, outside the ubiquitous chain link fencing Lally always thought to be such a blot on the landscape. Stopping the car, she took a look through the fence. A long narrow driveway led to a small house set well back, the attached garage lending a false sense of size. To the left of the drive was an unbroken wall of tall poplars, some of them dead and gray. To the right, close to the road, was an undistinguished-looking white dwelling stained with blown red dust.

She opened the gate in the wire fencing, which fastened inside with a simple hook-and-eye. She turned the car into the driveway, and went carefully along it. There was an attempt at minor ornament on both sides, long thin strips of white sweet alyssum edging the raggedy oblongs of lawn. On the whole, it didn't look the sort of place that would house a dog like Parma. However.

She stopped the car near the closed double doors of the garage, ran up her window so that Parma couldn't get out but could have an open six inches for air, and went briskly to the front door.

There was neither bell nor knocker. Standing on the doorstep, she heard through the closed wooden door music playing very loudly, radio or television, she didn't know which. She rapped twice with her knuckles, waited, and then thinking that Mrs. Cove probably couldn't hear her with all that noise going on, cogitated for a moment.

Mrs. Cove might be in her kitchen, or even napping in her bedroom. It was only her concern for the woman that took Lally around to the side of the house facing the wall of poplars.

The first window looked into a small living room. At the second, the curtains were drawn, leaving a center gap of only a few inches. Lally took a quick glance through the gap.

She saw a brass bedhead right against the window. She saw a woman's head on the pillow a few feet away. She saw, almost lost in deep shadow, a man's hands. The hands took the top edge of the sheet and drew the sheet over the woman's face and head. There was no sound, except the music playing. The window was open halfway.

She made a little involuntary sound herself, a half-gasp. The hands disappeared. For the life of her she couldn't take her eyes off the curtain gap. She apprehended rather than saw the man backing off a bit, standing very still, a mere sketch or suggestion of a man in a darkened room.

Move, get out of here, get away from whatever horror, or sadness, or tragedy she had just witnessed the very end of. A dead face being decently covered . . .

Resisting the impulse to run, she walked swiftly to the Volkswagen, got in, turned around in the limited space, and started the engine. Her hands were working but not her mind; she was still deep in shock.

She was a third of a mile down Mott Road when she realized she had forgotten to close the gate behind her. Did it matter? There had been no animal in sight to run out at the gate.

Parma seemed to sense something odd about her companion and edged closer, her muzzle heavy and warm on Lally's shoulder.

I don't think I'll stop for fruit after all, Lally thought. In fact, I'll be lucky if I make it home at all in this condition.

Along she drove, slowly, thirty miles an hour, drove wrapped inside nightmare.

## 15

Moving like a sleepwalker, Lally on returning to her house went into the kitchen. Her strict rule went unenforced: Parma lay in the center of the kitchen floor, watching her with interest while she cut butter into flour for her biscuit dough. The able, unthinking hands paused in their kneading. Strawberry shortcake, that was what she was making. But she had no strawberries and no heavy cream. She hadn't bought these two items.

She put the dough in a bowl in the refrigerator, and considered in a remote fashion what dinner tonight would consist of. There was a nice piece of round steak left from the Sunday breakfast cut, and three ripe tomatoes, maybe thinly sliced white onions with them, and rings of green pepper, a big platterful of that . . . and baked potatoes . . .

Her knees felt as though they were about to buckle under her when she bent to see if she had any potatoes in the bottom of the open bin, and her head swam, and the kitchen dimmed. Better get yourself off to bed, she ordered sternly. Take a couple of aspirins first.

She may or may not have slept fifteen minutes; she had gone to bed at four-thirty and the clock said four forty-six when she found herself staring at it. She couldn't back away from this thing forever. Try to think it out, and then put it away.

Start with the obvious and the least frightening. Against her will, her mind began working and probing. After a long illness, as lugubrious obituaries read, Mrs. Cove had quietly

and inevitably expired. Naturally the room would be darkened. Her husband, or a brother perhaps, sitting waiting for
the end, at the bedside. It comes. He covers her face.

But if this were so simply the case (people unfortunately
die very often every day everywhere) why all the commotion
about the missing spitz? And it had been Mrs. Cove, the dog's
owner, who had called the Humane Association in tears.

Why the telephone calls from her, Lally, left unanswered,
when there was someone in the house patiently watching and
waiting? Why the loud music, surely no comfort to one in
extremis?

Lally turned over on her other side. Suppose, in a last-
straw kind of way, the woman had committed suicide, the
missing dog providing the final tap of despair. A loved and
only companion, the spitz . . . But who then was the companion who had pulled the sheet over her face?

Or a careless and not deliberate overdose of drugs? It happened all the time.

She gave herself a few brief seconds to contemplate the
impossible. There was something about the secrecy, and the
darkness, and the music, and the man's absolute lack of response to the little cry she had uttered outside the window
. . . What if the man had killed her and just couldn't bear to
look at her face? A rejected or rejecting lover? Lally tried to
summon back an impression of the woman, any clue to her
age and looks, but only remembered the blondish messed-up
hair on the pillow and a nose, just an ordinary kind of nose.

It came to her—to her brain and her responding heart action—that if there had been any wrongdoing involved, any
act of violence, she had been standing there in the man's full
view, face very near the window, in that glaring gray afternoon light. While she had only seen a shadowy shape, he
must have gotten a complete, and unforgettable, picture of
her down to the last eyelash.

And the car had been standing very near the front door. A

dusty old anonymous car. But when she was turning it around he could have seen the license plate. She saw hands, the hands that had held the sheet, taking down, with pencil or ballpoint, on the back of an envelope, the Volkswagen's license number.

Nonsense, don't conjure up demons and dragons. If it was an ordinary death there would probably be a notice in tomorrow's or the next day's paper. If it had been the result of a sudden accident, on the road or at home, that might be in the paper too. But if it was a fatal accident why wasn't Mrs. Cove in the emergency ward of a hospital, instead of quietly dying in her own bedroom?

Maybe it wasn't Mrs. Cove at all, but a sister or a relative who lived with her. Lally provided the small house with a second bedroom, where Mrs. Cove would sleep. Maybe the whole thing had nothing whatever to do with Mrs. Andrew Cove herself. It was a thought to seize, develop, and cling to with both hands.

Of course. Of *course*. The body on the bed was not Mrs. Cove at all.

Nevertheless when the telephone rang she answered it in a voice that shook. Now, Mrs. Cove again, inquiring about her spitz . . . ?

It was a man's voice, strong, excited. Was he talking to Mrs. Thomas Hyde? He had just, he said, gotten back to town and called the Animal Humane people about a missing brand-new Samoyed, and they had reported her call to him. He had been gone since Sunday evening. A patient of his who summered in Colorado Springs had had a coronary and sent his private jet to Albuquerque to collect him. "I'm a doctor, a cardiologist," he explained. When he got home he found that his new dog had jumped over the fence, a five-foot-high fence, on Monday morning.

In a suddenly deflated tone, he said, "Before I phoned in

the ad to classified I thought I'd try you. I suppose her owner has turned up? I don't suppose she's my dog?"

"I'm afraid she's a spitz, owned by a woman named Cove," Lally said. "But I thought at first, too, that she might be a Samoyed. And yes, she's still here."

"Would you describe her, please? As I said, she'd just been delivered to me late Sunday afternoon, I hadn't even time to get her a leash and a collar, and she hasn't even a name, only her kennel name, Champion Crystal White Rose, of all the damn-fool things."

"She *is* a crystal white rose," Lally said, tears somewhere at the back of her throat, she didn't know why, weakness and a trace of aftershock, maybe. "Young, huge dark eyes, very fine silky long white eyelashes, plumy tail generally held down, not up, very heavy coat—"

"Oh my God," he interrupted. "I think, yes, I do think—although I can't quite believe it, I'd given her up—that it is my dog. May I come over and take a look? I'm only six or seven streets away, up and over from Andalusia. Of course it may be another dog from the same kennel." Obviously bracing himself for disappointment, he fell into a spate of words.

"My wife's off, visiting her parents in Pennsylvania, the dog was bought as a present for her. Our housekeeper is a very hardworking woman but not a deep thinker in emergencies. When she saw the dog jump the fence, she was afraid of calling what she terms the animal people because she thought it might be captured and taken to the pound, and she knew I'd spent a bundle on her. And the placement of a classified ad is entirely beyond her range. She kept hoping the dog would find her own way back. Did you say it would be all right if I came over now? My name, by the way, is Robert Everest."

"Yes, of course." Lally went into the bathroom and washed her face, which looked to her alarmingly pale and older than it ought to. She combed her hair, put on a little lipstick, crookedly, to brighten up the facial landscape, and over the slip she had lain down in put back the pants and shirt she had taken off. Parma followed her from the bathroom doorway to the bedroom.

"Come on," Lally said. "We'll go out and wait on the doorstep. In a way I hope it's your owner and in another way I hope it isn't." Still addressing Parma, she added, "I think Everest is a good name for a specialist, don't you, Parma? In reference to fees, I mean," and hearing herself, thought, Lord, is this hysteria? No, just the prospect, suddenly a bit bereaving, of losing Parma.

In ten minutes, a dark blue Cadillac drew up in front of the house. A man leaped out and stood by the low wall, gazing at the two on the doorstep. There was no mistaking the look on his pleasant pink-tan face: astonished wonder and joy.

Lally opened the driveway gate for him and he went swiftly to the dog and bent, stroking her head. She had gotten up and was waving her tail in a questioning way. "Miracles do happen," said Everest. "Oh my God, what a relief. Come on home, girl."

In the end, Lally had to hand-guide the rather unwilling Parma to the Cadillac, where a small boy on the back seat flung open the door. "After all, she's only known me a few hours and you for two whole days," Everest said, in half-apology for requiring her escort services. "Natural enough." Seeing the child, Parma got up a little enthusiasm and with a slight push from Lally jumped into the car.

"How can I thank you, what can I do?" the doctor asked.

"By keeping her the happy dog she is, I suppose," Lally said. "Her temporary name here was Parma. She was fond of lying on my violet bed near the step."

"Parma it will be then. May I replace your violets for you?"

"No, I've lots more in the back to fill in the crushed places."

"Goodbye then, and thanks again. I'll call the God-blessed Humane people as soon as I get home."

The Cadillac drove off and Lally went with tears on her cheeks into her empty house.

She decided not to tell Darrell about what she had seen at the house on Mott Road. It would mean that she would, in talking about it, have to relive it, and she didn't want that. A secondary reason, at this time, was that if something wrong or awful had been going on, she didn't want to involve him in possible if unlikely danger.

"Where's Parma?" he asked when he got home a little after six.

"Wonderful news," Lally said, having washed away her tears and brought herself to the conclusion that it was on the whole a good thing. "Her owner picked her up an hour or so ago. I've never seen a happier cardiologist."

Darrell gave her a sharp look, noting the shadowed eyes.

"She was nice for you to have around. Do you think it might be a good idea for you to take on a dog of your own?"

It occurred to him that a few days ago . . . a different world ago . . . the last thing he would have thought of doing was to recommend to Lally the company of a loving and protecting dog.

"I'll see how I get along without her . . . And did you finish up your greenhouse?"

"No, a couple of hours' work tomorrow, noonish I'd say, if he doesn't have a hundred errands to follow it up, the table, and getting clay pots and flats to plant in, and fitting hose connections."

It crossed Lally's mind that the bishop might very well, to keep her at bay, be busy right now on a list of greenhouse addenda. "Tell him you'll be able to offer him time on weekends, that your number one project is to find a good job as fast as possible."

"Did that man Duff call by any chance?"

"No, but he will, I know he will." Miracles, as Dr. Everest had said, do happen.

After dinner, Darrell spent an absorbed hour looking through his black-and-white shots of Jerome, which he had picked up at the drugstore on his way home. Lally tried to concentrate her wandering mind on her book. Neither of them was much interested in television; the set on its stand was kept pushed behind Tom's wing chair in the corner.

At a little after nine, she said, "I don't know . . . this close heavy weather . . . I think I'm off to bed."

"Good. You look tired. Don't forget your glass of port," Darrell said.

On Wednesday morning, after Darrell had gone off, Lally took a second cup of coffee into the living room and got her *Journal* off the doorstep.

Her eyes raked swiftly through its pages. She found it on page seven. "Mott Road Resident Found Strangled to Death."

She closed her eyes for a few seconds and then opened them.

"Mrs. Andrew Cove of 614 Mott Road was discovered dead in her bed late yesterday afternoon by a neighbor, Mrs. G. Gutierrez, who had come over from her house next door to borrow a quart of milk. According to police reports, Mrs. Cove was strangled to death at some time earlier in the afternoon. There were no signs of violence other than the strangling. Police say that the murderer must have pulled the top bedsheet up and over Mrs. Cove's face and head. Other neighbors on Mott Road are being questioned about possible afternoon visitors observed at the house, which is set well back from the road and completely concealed from the Gutierrez residence by a wall of poplar trees. Mrs. Cove's immediate neighbors on the other side, Mr. and Mrs. Edward Jones, were at work all day at their separate jobs, Mr. Jones returning home first at his usual hour of 5:45. The playgrounds and buildings of Mott Middle School, which is closed for the summer, occupy the opposite side of the road. Police are anxious to get in touch with Mr. Andrew Cove, the victim's husband, who is reported to be on a sales trip in the Midwest for his employers, Acme Tools, Inc., an Albuquerque concern."

## 16

Lally sat without moving in her chair for several minutes. She was aware, at first, of tight breathing and found herself drawing in gulps of air. The wind blew the curtain against the back of her head and her heart banged twice.

Her thoughts, when she was able in a fashion to think, were not in orderly cohesion but after a time formed a dimly readable pattern.

She had no intention whatever of going to the police and telling her story. It seemed to her that it might place her in terrible danger. She had no idea of the extent to which police protection of key witnesses went. If at all.

And she would have nothing to describe anyway. Nothing helpful. Nothing identifying. She racked her brains to seek out anything memorable about the man's hands—rings, the color of the hair on the back of them, the shape of the hands, square, or long and narrow? Tanned, or pale, or red?

No, of course she couldn't be of any help even if she was a much braver woman. She remembered nothing about the hands. Except—

An out-of-focus picture fleshed out memory a little. A recollection of one of the hands swiftly lifted to the place where a face would be. She studied this gesture now and thought, of course, the normal human shielding of tears; and then, no, not tears from a man who had strangled her.

Unless it wasn't he who had done it. Unless he had come in after the death and in ordinary decency pulled the sheet up.

Then why hadn't he, instead of Mrs. Gutierrez, quite a while later, reported it to the police?

The music. It must have been playing so loudly that if she cried out she couldn't be heard.

Light being what it was, mysterious and hard to calculate when you were bathed in it or sunk in shadow, she realized with a tingle at her scalp and fingertips that the man couldn't actually know how much or little she had seen of him. For all he knew, she might be able to describe him accurately. He would have been feeling, then and now, in a state of disastrous exposure.

What would he do about it?

If he had the license number, he could find out who owned the Volkswagen and head for the Martinez house. Warn Rose? "I heard there's a dangerous man prowling about in the neighborhood, don't open your door to any stranger." It was only the decent thing to do, as soon as she felt strong enough to reach for the telephone.

If, on an investigating journey in his car, the man turned his observation or even binoculars on the Martinez house and discovered that the woman outside the window on Mott Road bore no resemblance to Rose Martinez, he could have no idea who the driver was. It could have been anybody from anywhere in the city, borrowing Rose's car.

Her mind took a sharp and necessary turn up another route.

She decided that the only sensible thing for the man to have done in his situation was to get immediately out of town for the time being.

It was the only rationalization she could live with.

She couldn't, indefinitely, hide in her house. To avoid the eyes of a man driving by today, or next week, or next month. It was unthinkable. In any case, Darrell might suspect this strange reclusiveness, back her into a corner, get the story out of her, go to the police, and—No.

She made herself conclude that the last thing for the man to do would be to come within miles of her, and her recognizing eyes.

At eleven-thirty, Darrell gave a friendly pat to the pre-painted white aluminum door of the greenhouse, just fitted into place. He stepped back and regarded his work with satisfaction. It looked nice, and neat, and very useful, the greenhouse.

He began stamping the large cartons flat. He was a tidy workman and if he had a pickup truck would have taken the cartons off to the town dump, but the Pontiac wouldn't accommodate them. Instead, he would place them behind the two garbage cans in the Jerome garage, a detached adobe structure built in the northeast corner of the surrounding wall.

The kitchen door opened and, making heavy use of his stick, Percival Jerome came out. His appearance was a surprise. Instead of the natty knicker suit, he wore a gray wool bathrobe which looked to be an old one, certainly not up to his usual dress standards. His face looked gray too, under the surface pink.

"Very nice job, all done, I see," he said. "At least the basic part of it."

"Are you all right?" Darrell reached out a supporting hand.

"Just one of my off-off days. Yes, I'll take that arm, if I may, perhaps you'll help me back up to bed. I didn't want you darting off before we had a chance for a little conference about what's to be done next."

Darrell waited until Jerome was in bed, head and shoulders against two large pillows, before quoting Lally more or less word for word. ". . . but you see, my number one project is to find a good job as soon as possible, so until this weekend . . ."

Jerome took a sip of brandy from the glass on the bedside

table. "Naturally, one is last on everybody's list, in this condition," he said grimly. "Let Jerome fall where he may."

Not for the first time Darrell thought what a depressing and difficult housemate this must be, for Lydia.

"Well, I hope you'll be better soon." He turned to go and then said, "Can I bring you up something to eat, a cup of soup or something, some crackers?"

"No, thank you, my appetite is . . . let's not go into that. If Lally inquires about me, you might tell her I'm not at all well, and will spend the afternoon sleeping, or trying to."

There had been no mention of payment for his services, and Darrell felt disinclined under the circumstances to press the matter here and now. Was he to be kept waiting until the list of extra trimmings was completed? He didn't want any more donations from Lally, and he'd need money for his pursuit of a job. Call Lydia tonight. Dun poor Lydia.

When he arrived home and made his report, he was startled to hear Lally burst out, "That old devil! Sick in bed, is he?"

"You don't look all that well yourself," he said, concerned.

"I had trouble sleeping, one of those thrashy nights. How would you like a nice bacon and tomato sandwich? Russian dressing or mayonnaise?"

Aware that she didn't want to talk about her obvious indisposition, he said, "Russian. I'll go out and get some lettuce, shall I? It looks nice and tender."

After lunch, Lally said, "I'm going to need the car this afternoon, odds and ends to see to. The middle garden needs mowing and weeding and you'll probably want to get the phone if that man Duff calls."

Darrell heard but didn't hear. After she had gone, he went to the garage and from a miscellaneous collection of pieces of wood selected a fifteen-by-fifteen-inch square about two inches thick. In his bedroom, he placed the wood mount on the desk by the window and got his box of clay out of the closet. With his photographs spread over the remaining free space of the desk surface, he went, with a deep interest soon followed by a pleasant passion, to work.

He would rough out the basic shapes of the head and features and then (a feeling of silent strength rising within him) would tell Jerome that the time had come when he must sit for him.

As is often the case with friends given the freedom to come and go in each other's houses, Lally had a key to the Jerome house. She had suspected the front door would be locked and it was.

The living room was empty, pill bottles and brandy decanter missing from the table. On hearing of the bishop's having taken to his bed, she had made up her mind not to be balked but to go into immediate action. He could feign severe illness and the need for bed rest indefinitely.

Taking the stairs at leisure, husbanding her sudden shortage of breath, she paused outside his door. She knocked in no uncertain terms. "Percy!" she called crisply.

After a little silence, his voice, deliberately blurred, she suspected, said, "Lally? I'm not well. You woke me . . . Another time perhaps."

"Nonsense. If this is the way you're going to play it, we'll carry on the conversation through your closed door. I assume you can hear me?"

"I am not listening to you. As I have said, I am not at all well. I am half under sedation."

"Okay. But, no time like the present. I'll write out my suggestions downstairs and slip the paper under your door. All you have to do is drag yourself out of bed, and study them and think them over. You'll be able to grasp the matter clearly when you're out from under sedation. And by the way, I'd be careful about doping myself if I were you, alone in the house like this."

She went down to the living room and made for the flap-front desk. She found this locked and thought indignantly what a bore it must be for Lydia to have to ask for the key whenever she wanted a stamp or a bill which had to be paid, or any of the myriad things kept in desks. Then she remembered the paint-splashed writing table in Lydia's studio and sat down to it to compose her note.

She pondered for a moment. Her mind seemed to be every which way, but no wonder. She consulted, on the back of Tom's letter, the ideas she had put down on first reading it. Then, putting on her reading glasses, she set forth briefly the face-saving plan she had conceived, heir A or heir B unfortunately deceased and the Jeromes' resulting unexpected and ample inheritance. This took one fairly long paragraph, in her forceful if right now somewhat shaky hand.

The second paragraph was short and also very much to the point. She foresaw dithering, backing and filling on the bishop's part, and intended to dispense with any of this.

"I want to hear from you exactly how you intend to carry out this plan, as well as how soon. I can see no possible cause for delay. Deadlines are helpful to dilatory people. Your deadline is by the end of the day Saturday. The alternative is—and I don't care for threats—that I will plainly and simply show the letter in question to Lydia and let her take it from there. Yours, L."

She ran a powerful underline beneath the last sentence.

There was no necessity for an envelope; only his eyes would see this missive and she had no doubt that it would be burned or torn into confetti once he had read it. She marched up the stairs, slid it under the door, and gave the edge a shove. She knew there was no impeding carpeting because his bedroom had a specially laid skid-proof floor of expensive black and white plastic squares.

She knocked again, and said, "The mail's just been delivered, Percy," and turned and went down the stairs.

At six o'clock, Jack Rolt left the office of Double-Ace Quality Used Cars, the firm he owned, to head home. The lot was left to the care of his assistant Fred. It would be open as usual until ten o'clock. Fred was reasonably reliable, but on his hiring had gotten off an unfortunate remark. "Double-Ace? Funny name for this kind of a setup. It's so easy to nickname it Double-Trouble Used Cars." Rolt had decided to overlook it because these times it wasn't all that easy to find an all-right kid in his early twenties to serve as his assistant.

For his homeward journey, he selected a tan Ford pickup from the far end of the lot. There was nothing unusual in this; to save wear and tear on his platinum-gray Buick LeSabre, he put his own merchandise to work.

The day had been a severe strain, even though there wasn't a nibble on one car or truck all through it. He had been listening through every pore of his body all day long for the sound of a police siren, coming closer, siren turned off, patrol car rolling onto the lot. There had been neither near siren nor patrol car.

He was thankful that he'd be returning to an empty house. This was his wife Glorianne's Wednesday Spree, as she called it. An afternoon of the game Bingo-at-Home with seven or eight of her girlfriends, then merry rounds of ginger ale and Bourbon, then a potluck dinner which they all rather hazily cooked together. The party rotated from house to house. Not his house tonight, thank God.

The Rolt residence, which he never failed to survey without a flicker of pride, was in the Northeast Heights, at the base of the Sandias, where lots of real honest-to-God money lived. Most of the money in this case was his wife's, even though Rolt cleared a decent enough living from his business. But Double-Ace would not have paid for the large two-story pink-painted brick house, with its ell-shaped angling around an oval swimming pool edged in pink tiles, the swimming pool in the front yard so that everybody would know there was one, but half concealed by a row of Lebanon cedars trimmed to their sword-pointed tops by the twice-a-week gardener. It took Glorianne's deceased husband's chemical fertilizer money to pay for this kind of splendor.

Rolt drove the humble pickup the length of the thickly white-pebbled driveway to the three-car garage at the rear of the house. He went in through the kitchen, using his key. The maid-cook, Eleanora, wouldn't be around, another thank-God. Spree Wednesday was her weekday off. Behind the scarlet vinyl-covered bar in what his wife called the TV lounge, he picked up a bottle of scotch, poured himself a stiff drink, and carried it up to the master bedroom, which overlooked the pool.

He could relax for a while, or as far as anyone in his situation could relax, he amended. He figured twilight would be the best time, shadow time. That wouldn't be for another hour or so.

After he had had his drink, sitting in a deep chair and gazing down at the swimming pool, he went into the large master bathroom, lined with marble in Glorianne's favorite color, pink. He went to the oval double sinks in the marble counter under the wide mirror, hesitated, took a last view of the way he looked now, and shaved off the heavy mustache he had worn for the past five years.

Mustaches were fairly common, but still—no sense asking for it. Even if people couldn't see you too well, they might remember the thick dark horizontal stroke under the nose, the mustache.

He had thought about doing this on getting out of bed at seven but then thought that it might look funny if, the very morning that the item might appear in the paper, he had turned up markedly altered as to face. Glorianne would be annoyed, she liked his mustache, but he would tell her that he'd been feeling an itch underneath and worried about an infection starting. In fact, he would go to bed tonight with a heavy coating of cortisone ointment on his upper lip.

He changed into dark trousers and a dark blue shirt. He put on sunglasses, not his showy blue shading through beige ones but plain deep green. From a hook in the closet he took a duck-billed brown cotton cap. "You look so *common* in that cap," Glorianne always objected.

He took a look at the new model in the mirror. He thought that now he looked just about like anybody else, maybe a little better. The glasses hid his pale honey-hazel eyes and thick black eyelashes. Just a healthy joe in his mid-thirties, a little of the dark brown hair curling out from under the cap; he shoved the curls underneath. Taller than average but not that much taller.

He got his binoculars out of a drawer and looked at his watch. Her place, Rose Martinez's place, was about half an hour's drive away.

Time to start the ball rolling.

## 17

The premises across the street from the Martinez house would have pleased even a casual loiterer. A For Sale sign near the road was almost the only indication of a house, all but buried in a grove of Russian olive trees. A dirt lane ran up beside it. To its right was an immense field where horses grazed in the dusk, then stables, then distantly far right a large incongruous-looking—in this landscape—fake English Tudor house.

Rolt turned his car up the lane. The house for sale could be seen more clearly beyond the low stone wall along the lane. It was dark and he hoped empty; at this time of the evening, unless they were asleep or out, people would have their lights on. He drove past the house and found on his left a stand of piñon. He pulled the car off the lane onto grass, under the pines.

If anyone asked him what he was doing in the neighborhood, he had his answer ready. "Chavez Tree Service—job order to be looked over."

He walked down the lane and entered the grove of Russian olives near the Andalusia Trail corner. He was completely and comfortably screened. Turning around, he saw that unless he showed a light, flashlight or match, he couldn't be seen from the dark house either. He put his binoculars to his eyes and moved right into the Martinez house.

There, lights were on and shades were up at open windows. A fat bald man sat watching television, a can of beer at his elbow. Rolt could hear the sounds of the set, a show Glori-

anne liked to watch, *Millionaire's Row*. The man drained his
can and called, "Rose!"

Rolt stiffened. Because he could so easily expose and ex-
plore this house, these people, he felt exposed himself. What
he was up to was dangerous but it would be a good deal more
dangerous if he wasn't.

From the kitchen doorway a woman came into the front
room, carrying another can of beer. Rose, right. Martinez,
right. She was the wrong woman.

She was short and dark-haired, fortyish, anything but el-
derly. Her coloring was vivid. She wore a bright red dress.
She placed the can of beer beside the man who might be Mr.
Martinez or a friend.

Shock hit Rolt squarely in the ribs. He swung his invading
lenses to the left of the house, the driveway, where near the
open doors of the garage the black Volkswagen was parked.
Light from a side window showed him the license plate, the
right numerals and letters on it, unmistakable.

Maybe the Martinez's next-door neighbor had borrowed
the car? Probably too simple, too easy. He swung his binoculars farther to the left and in a minute or so visually entered
the living room of the adobe house. In a minute or so, the
lamps were switched on, showing him a man who looked
thirtyish, slim but strong build, copper-burned skin and
shiny black hair cut smart-ass Eastern, in a loose not very
long bell. He too had a can of beer in his hand. He moved to a
place to which vision was blocked, sitting down in a chair no
doubt.

Then a woman came into the room and Rolt was shocked
back to the dark bedroom, the music, the body on the bed
whose contorted face he could not bear to look at.

Square shoulders, dust-colored short hair, ruddy skin. The
woman complete in every detail, the right woman. Late sixties or well-preserved early seventies.

The woman sat down in a chair not far from the two front

windows of the room. She took the newspaper off the table beside it and then with one hand fumbled the table's surface. Looking for eyeglasses? A brief domestic hunt got underway, the young man prowling about, the woman vanishing through a doorway and then coming back, shrugging. She sat down again and opened the paper, squinting and frowning at the type.

Rolt had examined the afternoon paper himself and she wouldn't find much in the way of an update, just a rehash. Police now sifting and collating information gathered about Tuesday afternoon's comings and goings in the murdered woman's neighborhood. Police still eager to contact Mr. Cove, who hadn't been in touch with his home office for several days, but Acme said that was not in any way unusual. Mr. Cove never left behind him a formal itinerary but usually felt his way around his sales loop when traveling.

Who, Rolt asked himself, was the man? He looked too young to be her son. Did he live there or was he visiting? Did he work? Nights, days, or not at all? He seemed very much at home. Did anyone else live there? Was there a husband?

There was motion in the living room again. The man passed the window to the left and as he opened the front door the woman called, "You won't forget to lock up when you get back? Do you expect to be late?"

"With my luck, no," the man said, laughing. He went to the garage, backed the car out, and drove off. The woman sat very quietly for a moment in her chair and then got up and pulled the shades on the front windows to the sills.

Rolt had no way of knowing whether the man had gone off on a ten-minute errand or a jaunt of several hours. And no way of knowing if there was anyone else in the house.

It was just a matter of waiting, and thinking of ways and means. It might take quite a few late evenings and early nights here under the enshrouding trees.

HIS money: it was as good an excuse as any for seeing Lydia, and he didn't want any more handouts from Lally.

She answered his knock and said, "Hello, come on into the kitchen, I'm just finishing up the dishes."

"Can I dry them for you?"

"No, thanks." Too close, too homey an arrangement for her?

He sat down at the table. Be forthright about it. The laborer worthy of his hire and all that. "The reason I came," he began, "or at least one of the reasons . . ." The role of bill collector suddenly appeared unattractive. "I like your shorts." Hazy blue and gray madras, a shirt to match, the sleeves rolled up over slender golden-beige arms. "I know your father has a lot more things he wants done in the greenhouse, so maybe . . . but . . ."

"Do you always handle your business dealings this way?" She turned from the sink laughing, but nicely laughing. "You've done three days' hard work and it looks very shipshape, I must say. What do we owe you?"

"Two and a half days. At six dollars an hour, a little over twenty hours, a hundred and twenty-six dollars. I have a note here for the times I began and stopped each day." He reached into his pocket.

"Don't be ridiculous. Do you want a check or cash?"

Darrell smiled. "Do *you* always handle business this way? I'll leave my work sheet on the table for your father anyway, in case he wants it."

He felt that there was an unseen warmth around him here in the kitchen, having nothing to do with the temperature. But maybe all kitchens felt that way.

She said, "Suppose I pay you out of what after all is really your money—you wrung it or rather almost hammered it out of your brother on my behalf. I was keeping it in an envelope thinking I'd mail it back to him. I haven't gotten around to that yet."

"It's not mine, it's yours. But knowing the original source, it will be even nicer to spend."

Counting out his money in the studio, she asked, "How's the bust coming along? Or haven't you started?"

"Oh, yes, I've started. Just, though." She looked in surprise at a different Darrell, the eyes irradiated, the face glowing with a form of strength. And something she had never felt in his presence before: the power of confidence flowing from him.

". . . and one dollar makes twenty-six. You haven't included tax."

"To hell with the tax. Now may I spend some of this on you? Will you come out and play?"

"Sorry, I'm really stuck here tonight." She always fought the long-suffering ways of the victimized daughter; her voice was calm. "Father's either worse than usual or in a stew or both. You and he didn't quarrel, did you? Something's upset him but it's hard to tell if it's a flea about to bite or a lion ready to spring on him."

"No, but he looked . . . well, bathrobe and all, and staying in bed like that . . ."

As she was putting the envelope with the money in it back into the table drawer, Lydia's eye fell on a pair of glasses beside a mugful of watercolor brushes. She picked them up, recognizing the frame shape and color, a light tortoise with a bent pin holding one earpiece to the right lens.

"These are Lally's," she said, in a puzzled way that Darrell didn't understand. Lally seemed to him a woman who would leave glasses and other oddments here, there, and everywhere.

"I'll take them back to her."

"But they weren't here this morning," Lydia said. "The table was a mess and after breakfast I tidied it up. She must have stopped around here today. I suppose he just told her to go away."

Darrell took the glasses from her hand and put them in his shirt pocket. Now, right this minute, before his glow faded . . . He put his arms around her and kissed her with great tenderness, very lightly, feathering his lips against hers; not as a matter of technique but because this was the way, the right way, you first held and kissed your Lydia.

Then he dropped his arms before anything could be said to undo what felt like a spell to him, said, "Well, good night, I hope your father is better tomorrow," and went into the hall and down the front steps, forgetting to close the door behind him.

Lally was glad that the long night was behind her, its shallow sleep pierced here and there with awareness. A passing car, slowing, why? A drunken shout from another car, the sound of a beer can thrown out of its window hitting the slates. A distant rooster not greeting the dawn but forecasting it well in advance.

Return to her firm conclusion: that the man would have no choice but to leave town, the man with the hands.

The brilliant morning was reassuringly anticlimactic, comfortingly prosaic. She and Darrell agreed at breakfast that the engine of the car was sounding not only old but odd and she asked him to take it for a checkup at the garage she favored on Osuna Street.

"I suppose I should be thinking of a new car, or rather a good used one, but with Joan and her money problems . . ." She felt too weary to press Joan at the moment. Darrell wasn't listening to her anyway.

He had been up since six, at work with his clay. He thought that if Jerome was better today he'd go over and squeeze a sitting out of him. In the meantime he would see about the Pontiac's troubles.

Lally got three phone calls during the morning and each time picked up the receiver with a hesitation close to fear.

Mary Cronin, a friend of hers, wanted her recipe for cheddar cheese crust for an apple pie she was going to make.

The second was to remind her that she had a four o'clock appointment at Dr. Wister's the next day, Friday, to have her teeth cleaned.

The third was from a research company whose name she didn't catch, something-or-other Media Surveys, a man's voice. Would she be kind enough to answer a short questionnaire on television viewing? "I'm not much good to you, I hardly ever look at it," Lally said, "but go ahead, if it is short." First, how many in the household, sex and age? "We'll say I'm over sixty. I have a nephew staying with me, thirty. That's it." What daytime programs did they watch? None. What evening programs? "The news, not local, national, CBS, but only once or twice a week." What nighttime programs? "Only *Masterpiece Theatre*, Sundays, if I'm up that late." She was given a polite "Thank you, madam, for your cooperation."

Darrell thought that Jerome might by four-thirty have completed his nap, and dialed the number. When Jerome answered with a heavy "Yes?" he asked politely about his health. "A bit better, or marginally so." Was he well enough to sit, this evening, for a bit of modeling? "I fear that might be impractical."

Jerome seemed to fall to musing aloud. "I usually find it very tiring, managing for myself. It's Lydia's night for her private lessons to the Farquhar girls, she dines there first, Eleanor Farquhar, an old friend of hers, tennis and all sorts of frivolities beforehand, and then no doubt cocktails on the terrace . . . I've almost forgotten the joys of running about doing nothing. Or almost nothing—she's well paid for her lessons. I, on the other hand, will sit down to a cold dinner." He neglected to add that the morosely mentioned dinner, prepared in the afternoon by Lydia, was breast of chicken with lemon mayonnaise, tomato aspic, and his favorite blanched asparagus tips.

Fifteen minutes later Darrell got a call from Don Duff. "Can you pop over to my house eight-thirtyish?" Yes, Darrell could. "I'd better give you the directions, I'm a bit hard to find." There was a piece of scratch paper by the telephone with a scribble of Lally's on it. Darrell turned it over to the blank side and wrote down Duff's directions. "There's a misleading dead-end sign as you turn into Sierra, but turn in anyway, take your first left and then your first right. You pass a million-dollar setup that isn't mine, white with arches and fountains and peacocks, and two houses past it is a humble dwelling painted pale blue, which *is* mine." Darrell said he'd be there, and put the folded directions into his pocket.

Not knowing whether Duff was a far-out type or not, he put on the new white duck pants he had bought this afternoon with fifteen dollars of his greenhouse money, his tattersall shirt, and another afternoon purchase, red espadrilles. Lally, looking him over after dinner, said, "You look better, and not just the clothes, than I've ever seen you look in your life, young Darrell. Good luck. In case you're late, I'll lock up. Keys in the usual place."

Darrell didn't know what the usual place was, his possibly being out after Lally's bedtime not having occurred before. Lally told him.

Ten minutes after the Pontiac, its engine breathing restored almost to normal by the garage mechanic, left the driveway, the man across the street under the Russian olives saw with his binoculars a little storytelling incident.

The front window shades were swiftly pulled to the sills. From under the shade of the window nearest the door a forearm emerged. A hand holding a ring of keys dropped the keys into the window box, behind down-cascading sweet peas. Then there was the sound of the window being firmly closed.

Don Duff was a genially plump short man who looked to be in his early forties, with exuberant bright blue eyes and receding red-fair curly hair. Meeting Darrell at the door, he put a finger to the nearly bare crown of his head. "Television, I'd have to have a hairpiece. Radio, no. Good evening to you. You look okay and you haven't got two heads after all, although later I thought if you had you could give off a terrific double-voice effect. Come on in. The place is a mess, no little woman to tidy up, two divorces, that's enough, I say."

Darrell, sitting down on the sofa in the small cluttered living room, accepted a cold can of beer, and without nervousness or apology said what he had planned to say. "Point number one, I have no experience whatever in radio or TV."

"So what—at least you don't have somebody else's misguidance to unlearn. And you've got the voice. Who do you remind me of?" He snapped his fingers. "That guy Hyde, Tony Hyde, filming on location here, I caught him on the late news a few nights back. Voice like yours, looks something like you, only, excuse the expression, times ten. Related? Cousin? Brother?"

"Brother."

"Then what are you doing batting around here in the little leagues? Well, I'll say it before you do, none of my business."

He leaped to answer his ringing phone. (It rang eleven more times while Darrell was there.) After telling whoever it was at the other end that he'd see her probably before ten, sweetie, Duff brought a tape recorder to the coffee table and plugged it in.

"Don't pay any attention when the phone rings, it always does, I'll read out the rings when I'm playing you back. Here, do these if you will." He handed Darrell an untidy sheaf of papers, the portions to be read aloud circled in red ink. Three or four sixty-second commercials, a photocopy of Walter de la Mare's "The Listeners," six news items from the afternoon paper, two weather reports, a portion of an article on ancient

Egypt on a page torn out of *Smithsonian* magazine, and the twenty-second gospel of St. Matthew, verses 35–46.

Darrell read steadily on, having adjusted after the second blast of the telephone to the background commotion.

When he had finished, Duff took the receiver off the hook, picked up the tape recorder, and carried it into his bedroom. "Get yourself another beer from the fridge, I will listen to you in solitude," he said, and closed the bedroom door.

Duff came out after fifteen minutes. "Good pacing, a little fast but that's easily taken care of. Good accent—none. Good pronunciation—how come you don't pronounce 'nuclear' 'nucular' like half the U.S.? No lisp or potatoes in the mouth, although some TV big shots seem to get away with it."

Sitting down, he returned to his unfinished scotch and water. "And seeing I deliberately didn't give you any chance for rehearsing anything, good show. I may have to start you off on a free-lance basis, and then see how and where you can fit in, but you can consider yourself formally as part of the team at station KRCW. Come on around to the office at ten tomorrow and we'll discuss terms."

In his exhilaration, and his unfamiliarity with the neighborhood, Darrell took a wrong turning and soon discovered he was lost. After fifteen minutes of trying this road, and then that, he stopped at a gas station and asked the way to Andalusia Trail. He was given directions, and when the attendant came to ". . . will lead you into Rio Grande Boulevard . . ." Darrell said, "Thanks, I know my way from there."

Shortly after reaching Rio Grande, he saw about eighty yards ahead Lydia's Toyota turning in to the driveway opening in the adobe wall. He was tempted to stop, and rush in, and tell her about his interview. It was a quarter to ten by his watch, not late for her but her father might have taken pills or capsules to compose himself for sleep. And perhaps she would be tired after tennis and drinks and art lessons. He had once been pretty good at tennis; he thought that in between station KRCW and Jerome's head he might brush up his game at a YMCA court, if there was one here.

When he got back to Lally's, he noticed while putting the car away that only one room was lighted, the kitchen, the rest dark. She must have locked up and gone off to bed and left the one light on to invite him to get himself something to eat, cookies and milk, before he went to bed.

He reached behind the sweet peas in the window box for the keys, lit a match to see which one bore the bit of tape with "F" penciled on it, and opened the door.

He went to his right, into the living room, only marginally illuminated through the drawn shades by the lights in the Martinez house.

He tripped over something and fell, sprawling hard, on the rug. He made a half-yelping animal noise, hauled himself to his feet with a dreadful foreknowledge, and switched on the lamp beside Lally's armchair.

She lay on the rug, one leg at a strange angle, head twisted sideways, an awful eye open, the tongue—

He bent, in a panic entirely without hope, to the wrist, the pulse, and then fumbled for where the human heart might be supposed to be, to beat. Nothing. But her flesh was still warm.

There was a knock at the front door. Some kind of medical help called by someone, maybe after all not too late, artificial respiration—

But she's been strangled, he thought, sleepwalking to answer the door. He had never seen a strangling victim but he had read about the eyes, the tongue.

He opened the front door to Rose Martinez. She asked anxiously from the doorstep, "Is everything all right? I heard her maybe twenty minutes ago screaming your name, 'Darrell, *Darrell.*' I thought it might be a family fight, we have them over at our place, I thought I'd mind my own business but then I got to worrying. Is everything all right?"

## 18

"Okay," Lieutenant Garcia said. "Let's go through it again. Step by step, take your time."

"*Again.*"

"Yes, there might be some little thing you missed first time around, or something you forgot. Begin with when you sat down to dinner and what you ate, you and she."

Darrell and Garcia were sitting at the kitchen table. The policeman was thin and dark, youngish, with a Spanish music to his voice. In Tom's lighted office, another policeman was busily searching.

Darrell could never remember afterward who had called the police, he or the Martinez woman. After "Is everything all right?" she had taken a look at his face and gone into the living room. Behind her, he exploded in tears of grief and shock, his whole body shaking. She screamed, blessed herself four times, and screamed again.

And now here they were, the two of them, in the kitchen. The Martinez woman had been escorted weeping to her own house. There were men in the living room, flashbulbs going, puffs of fingerprint powder, all the scene-of-the-crime procedure going full blast over—all too vivid before Darrell's eyes —the terrible silent watching face on the floor.

At the beginning of his questioning, Garcia had eyed Darrell's unmarked face and throat. Then: "What's that scratch on the back of your right hand?" "Garden work a few days back, a rosebush." Garcia's eyes had moved thoughtfully to a pair of rubber gloves by the sink, used by Lally when doing the dishes. He got up and pocketed the rubber gloves.

It wasn't until later that Darrell saw the point of all this: his looking for visible marks of Lally's fight against death, her fight with *him* against death.

"We had dinner at seven. Chicken pot pie and a plain salad, just oil and vinegar dressing. Coffee and cookies. Spice cookies." With his handkerchief, he wiped sweat and tears off his face. "I left here at eight for an eighty-thirty appointment." Duff's name and address again, description of the interview again, details of getting lost, again. Again, Lally fine when he left, saying she might lock up early and go to bed, keys in the usual place, the window box nearest the front door. Then coming home, getting the keys out from behind the sweet peas, opening the door and falling over his aunt in the living room. No, he hadn't noticed any car lights, or motorcycle, or even bicycle, going away from the house in either direction.

"So the house was locked and only you and your aunt knew where the keys were?"

"Oh, come off it," Darrell said wearily. "Friends know other friends' habits. And people, anybody, people lift keys from handbags or pockets or see them lying around on tables, there's nothing to having keys copied . . ."

Again, list of what friends and acquaintances of Lally's Darrell knew about, and her relationships with them. "But I only got here last Thursday, so that . . ."

"What brought you out here? You get here Thursday, she's killed the following Thursday. Did you have some kind of a premonition, did you hear she was sick, or frightened of something, or been threatened by someone, or what?"

"No. I couldn't find work in the East, I like it here and we're fond of each other. I thought she'd give me a roof while I looked for a job, and she did."

On and on. How come he couldn't find work in the East, did he have a prison record, or bad reputation, or what?

Christ, Darrell thought suddenly, wait till they find out about my family, which of course they will, the hundreds of thousands, the millions of dollars in the heaped-up Hyde resources. While the youngest member of the family, an out-of-work drifter, goes two-thirds of the way across the country to pay a visit to an elderly aunt who lives alone.

And: *Say, this is too good to be true. It turns out he's her heir, lock, stock, and barrel.*

After Rose Martinez had got her sobbing at least partially under control, and with her husband sitting scowling by her side on the sofa, Sergeant Limmon returned to a matter of which he had gotten only hysterical snatches. "So about twenty minutes before you went over to the house—?"

"I heard Lally scream or shout twice, 'Darrell, Darrell.' Well, you know how it is, Joe here will come at me with a raised fist or something—"

"Hey!" her husband interrupted furiously.

"—and I'll scream and yell holy murder, that kind of thing goes on in families. I didn't want to butt in, it looked like they'd been getting along fine, so I thought, Let them settle it between themselves, maybe he just accidentally broke a vase or lamp or something. But then, the house was so quiet, and the living-room lights went out, and I got this funny scared feeling, and Joe said keep your nose out of other people's business and I went over anyway."

"Before you heard the screaming, you didn't see any strange car in front of the house, any stranger, say, loitering across the street, anyone going into the house?"

"No. But if you'll look out that side window, you can see that the juniper hides the front door and pretty well this whole side of her front yard from us. She never turns on her door light, she figures it's a signal to anyone that she's home alone."

"The nephew claims he just got there a minute or so before

you did, put the car away and unlocked the door and went in."

"That's easy," Joe Martinez said, jumping into the act. "He kills her, takes the car out for a bit, comes back and tries to make it look like he just discovered her stone dead."

"Did you see or hear him take the car out shortly before your wife went over?"

"Nah, TV, and I don't take all that much interest in people's comings and goings."

"Let's run through it again," said Lieutenant Nichols in a small interview room at the police station, where Darrell had been taken in a patrol car and fingerprinted. A policeman in a corner took shorthand notes.

In numbed, frail defiance, Darrell said, "I suppose by this time you've checked with Don Duff to find out if I was there this evening."

"Yeah. Naturally. Go ahead. From the beginning."

"My aunt and I had dinner at seven." Nichols had a sheaf of typed notes before him which he consulted between raking blue glances into Darrell's eyes. And on. And on. Forever, he would be telling this story, which began with chicken pot pie. Just slip a quarter in the slot and hear the man speak. Hear the man go step by step through the evening. Hear the man tell about how he read commercials, and a poem of Walter de la Mare's, and all that interesting stuff. He asked for a glass of water and was given one. Hear how the man got lost. Sounds suspicious, doesn't it? What a good night to get lost on.

"What was the gas station you asked directions at?"

"I told your other man, Garcia, I can't remember. Exxon and Gulf are all one to me."

"Yeah. I see that, here. Too bad. But then you're not a resident, came out here just a week before this happened."

At twelve forty-five, he read over his transcribed statement and signed it. Then, to his dulled astonishment, he was told he was being released pending further investigation. He was driven home in the patrol car. The police lock was removed from the front door and he was in the house, and alone.

Lally would have been taken away long ago. He lit one lamp and looked, blinking, around the empty, God how empty, living room. A thorough search had obviously been made, everything put back in its place, almost, an inch off in position here, two inches off there.

He went into his searched bedroom, took off his clothes, went into the searched bathroom, and back into the hall to lock and bolt the front door.

Getting into bed, he prepared himself for a grim and endless white night and fell almost immediately into the deepest and darkest sleep.

While the coffee was brewing, Lydia went at seven-thirty to pick up the morning paper from the path. She yawned her way back to the kitchen; she had stayed until one at the Farquhars, long after the lessons were over, because she enjoyed the couple's company and they hers, and it was she who had to remind Neil that it was high time he dropped her back at home.

She never took the car out for these pleasantly long sessions at their house because there was always the one chance in a hundred that the phone might go out of service, as infrequently happened, that her father would be stranded and helpless. This was what, among other crises, her occasional compelling him to the wheel was all about.

She had taken a third grateful swallow of the reviving fresh coffee when, casually turning the pages of the paper, she saw it. "Mrs. Thomas Hyde Victim in Violent Death on Andalusia Trail." She read it through a blur of unbelief, the short and factual story. The body had been discovered on the living-room floor by Mrs. Hyde's nephew, Darrell Hyde, who was currently residing with her. He had been out for an evening appointment and, returning, found his aunt strangled to death. The approximate time of the death had not yet been established. Mr. Hyde asserted that his aunt was alive and well when he left the house at eight o'clock for his appointment. Mrs. Hyde had been a longtime resident of Albuquerque. Her deceased husband had been with a local firm of accountants, Boone and Boone. The police were pursuing their inquiries.

Et cetera.

Other et ceteras moved unbidden into Lydia's appalled mind.

Tony asking about buying the chest in Lally's hall and she saying that Lally might not want to sell bits and pieces of the house now because . . . And Tony's swift and cynical response, "Her heir. Darrell." Each word came back to her. "Which is why I wasn't all that surprised to find he'd left mending nets or painting hulls or whatever he could find in Rockport to do—for fairer fields."

Yank your mind back from this. Lally had no enemies, no neighborhood quarrels. It must have been robbery with violence, Lally resisting the robber or robbers . . .

There was no account, in this first report, of anything being stolen from the house.

Roaming again, her mind, or not roaming, frantically flying around, trying to escape seeing things and hearing things. Darrell in the hall still holding a claw hammer in his hand. "You will take the money, because to get it for you I've drawn a nice picture of myself as a dangerous madman."

There was no mention in the third of a column devoted to Lally of an arrest. Darrell, then, was presumably home. Should she call him? What do you say to someone whose aunt has just been strangled? The aunt being your own good friend?

Unable to carry all by herself the burden of shock, and dawning loss and pain, she poured a cup of coffee for her father and brought it up, with the folded-back newspaper, on a little tray. To her light knock, he said, "Come in, though I've just barely opened my eyes."

Putting the tray on his bed table, she sat down, before her legs let go, in the flowered armchair.

His reaction as he read the news story seemed strange; but then anybody's would be. The widening blue eyes, the face flooded with a startled pink—he looked like a great glossy baby over whose crib an unexpected new object had been dangled. Dear God, he wasn't going to have a heart attack, was he?

"I should have prepared you, but I couldn't—" It was hard to see through the haze of tears in her eyes.

"Monstrous," her father said in a voice just above a whisper. "Monstrous. Lally of all people, good Lally." He went on with his solemn verbal obituary, most of which Lydia didn't hear, until he said, "You don't think that that nice young man—I believe he was her heir . . ."

Lydia said, "Are you *mad?*"—furious because of her own first, terrifying musings. How many people, she thought—instantly supplying the answer: hundreds and hundreds of people—would automatically, privately, bring to trial and condemn Darrell Hyde?

Until the police found out who really strangled Lally, that is.

The first telephone call from the press came at seven, waking Darrell from the bottom of his pit of sleep. He said, "I've got nothing to tell you that I haven't already told the police," and hung up. After a moment's thought, he took the receiver off the hook. He went and got the morning paper on the doorstep and found that he had been correct in his assumption: the story had been released, the factual bare bones of it, the account he had given to the police. Given four times in a row to the police.

The idea of going back to sleep wasn't workable. He was surprised to feel nothing, nothing at all, as though suspended in some kind of emotional void, a silence of the mind and the heart and the nerves.

He made coffee and, hearing a knock at the door, decided to ignore it. The knocking went on. Ten, twenty knocks. He stood just inside the closed and locked wooden door. A man's voice outside called, "Hey, Hyde! Can you hear me? Your brother sent me, your brother Tony. He thought you might need a hand."

Was this a fake, a reporter trying to get in? Darrell opened the door a cautious couple of inches and saw through the screen door a big man with a prizefighter's build, wearing jeans, sunglasses, and a raw-silk shirt.

"Mike Kaplan," he said. "You don't have to bother with any host-guest stuff. My orders are to sit out in front in the car and give the bum's rush—politely—to anyone coming around for interviews or photographs or scenes of grisly death and whatnot. You're under sedation and have no comment for the press or anybody else, okay?"

It seemed quite clear to Darrell that it was Tony Hyde whom Tony was protecting, and the other Hydes. In case his brother might make a headlining damned fool of himself one way or another, floods of tears, a confession to the first friendly caller, any half-assed thing that seized him at any given moment.

Feeling as he did, still inside his own echoing vacuum, he could summon no rage or defiance. "Suit yourself," he said, and turned away from the door. Mike Kaplan called after him, "Tony's coming along sometime this morning."

Tony arrived at eleven to find him sitting at the kitchen table staring at a cup of cold coffee. His presence was an unreal one in the quiet, clean room. Very short chino shorts, a persimmon-colored shirt, Roman sandals wrap-strapped up his handsome calves; only Tony, Darrell thought at a tangent, could get away with those.

"Whatever mood you're in, haul yourself out of it," Tony said crisply. "Relax. If and when they charge you we'll get you the best lawyers. You have absolutely nothing to worry about. I called the old man this morning, the purse strings will be untied when necessary."

It was then that Darrell started coming back to life, blood flowing in his veins, breath in his lungs. Tony, it seemed to him, either took it for granted that he had killed Lally or thought that it didn't matter whether he had or he hadn't, it was the family escutcheon that mattered.

Tony got up, flung open cabinets, found the bottle of scotch, got out ice, and poured two strong drinks. He placed one in front of Darrell and applied himself to the other.

"Don't move an inch from your story," he said, or rather ordered. "You got lost, which takes care of the time lapse. Of course, they'll be combing the gas stations around there wanting to know if you really did stop and ask directions." He fell into a musing tone as he examined probable investigations now going on. "They'll be checking your criminal record back East—have you ever been in jail, by the way?"

"No."

"That's more than I can say. But that was long ago. They'll be plowing into any history of drugs. And speaking of drugs, seeing by the autopsy results whether she was drugged at dinnertime, to make it easier for you to . . ."

Darrell began to shake. He reached for his drink and couldn't hold it against his clattering teeth. He threw it, glass and all, at Tony and watched the persimmon shirt turn dark where the liquor spread.

He stood up and said, "Get out of here. *Get out.*" He picked up the chair he had been sitting on. Was it in self-defense? He wasn't sure. Tony looked dangerous.

But in the calmed soft voice useful when addressing the

hysterical, Tony said, "Naturally you're beside yourself. Who wouldn't be? I'm leaving for the Coast early this afternoon, all finished up here. I would have gone this morning but I wanted you to know we're with you, financially, legally, and you'll be gotten off the hook."

He finished his drink and got up. From his billfold he took a slip of paper and put it on the table. "My home number, unlisted, and my office number. I'm geographically speaking your nearest if not your dearest."

Taking a clean kitchen towel off the rack, he gave the front of his shirt a swab. "In case you're tempted to throw a drink at a policeman, my impulsive friend, I'd think twice about it. And speaking of throwing, it's fortunate that there wasn't a hammer involved last night."

In the doorway, he paused for a moment and looked back. "Mike will be on duty all day, you can't do anything about that except thank me. Give my regards to that nice little artist girl, what's her name? Lisa. See you," and he was gone.

At eleven o'clock the telephone rang. Darrell had restored it to life ten minutes before, thinking that the police might be trying to get in touch with him and would rage officially at cut-off communication.

" 'Ere, wot's-all-this?" inquired a voice in imitation of the British bobby's traditional opening question. Darrell after a few seconds recognized Don Duff's voice at the other end.

"Your line's been busy. I expected you tennish until I finally caught a moment with the morning paper."

Another, if very small, drain opened to go down into. Goodbye, station KRCW.

"Of course, the police have been around to see you," Darrell said.

"Last night and again this morning, a few minutes ago. I told them all about our interview session and even offered to play the tape for them. They didn't say, last night, by the way, what you'd gotten yourself into, but I figured it was heavy trouble. I also told them that twice right after I moved in I got lost myself, trying to get home. I didn't tell them it was after partying."

"Well, thanks."

"Don't sound so final. We'll wait a few days. You don't come across to me as anybody's role model for murderer, as I avowed to them this morning. From what I've seen, in cases like this, they usually find the guy fast, or never. But it wouldn't look good if you were pinched on the air right in the middle of a commercial. Let's say, pending future events, we earmark ten on Monday morning for our sign-up. By the way . . . I'm terribly sorry about your aunt."

Among the readers of the Albuquerque newspapers—or those readers who took an interest in sudden and violent deaths—the reactions were pretty well shared.

"There's nothing about a robbery. Of course he did it, the nephew. Lost on the way home!"

When in the afternoon paper Tony Hyde's name appeared, "dynamic writer-director who has just concluded filming a sequence of his new movie, *The King's Peacock*, here," the probable guilt of the nephew got an extra, cynical fillip. "Well, with high-ups in the family, chances are that no matter what the truth is you can wriggle out of anything."

## 19

Lydia, tired of what she termed hiding in the underbrush, ashamed of what she called her own cowardice, picked up the telephone and called Lally Hyde's number, only it wasn't hers anymore. She got a busy signal, went without hesitation to the garage, and backed the car onto Rio Grande. Driving to Lally's house, she was aware of some small object pressing into the end of her spine.

When she stopped the car in front of the house, she got out and took a look at the crease between the driver's seat and the back cushion. She picked up the small object, a half-pint sterling silver flask engraved with the initials PJ. She stared at it and put it into her handbag. No clear conclusions offered themselves in a world which had, overnight, turned itself upside down, Lally dead, murdered, a thunderclap word which had never appeared in her personal vocabulary until now.

The flask, however, sent one message to the mind: her father must have taken the car out last night. It hadn't been there when she drove home yesterday afternoon.

There was another car parked in front of hers, a Honda station wagon. A large heavily muscled man walked up to her. Police? Plainclothes police?

"I'm a friend, Mike Kaplan," he said. "Just to see Darrell Hyde isn't pestered, press and stuff, rubberneckers."

"I'm a friend too," Lydia said. She moved firmly past him and crossed the slates to the door. Darrell immediately opened the screen door to her knock. She looked at his face and looked away from it, it wrenched and hurt her, whatever had happened to his face.

"Come in," he said. "I'm glad you—" And then going a deep red, "Why aren't you in school?"

"No classes today. I came over to . . . is there anything I can do?"

He wanted desperately to put his arms around her but didn't. He reached out and touched the back of her hand with two of his fingers. Something rushed pouringly up in Lydia: perhaps it was faith. She took his head in her hands and kissed him, swiftly and sweetly.

Darrell went straight to the core. "You don't think I killed her?"

"No. Never. Never, never."

"Help me, Lydia. I think everyone else thinks I did. But . . . oh, can I get you some coffee?"

"No, let's sit down, my knees keep feeling funny."

They sat side by side on the sofa in the living room, Darrell holding her hand as if it was his only anchor. "You know her friends, enemies, problems, maybe secrets. I know you were close."

"As far as I know, Lally had no enemies. And if she had secrets they were secrets from me too."

He hesitated and then said, "I found one secret. I was going through her handbag looking for God knows what, a threatening letter, a note of some kind. I found this"—getting up and taking a folded sheet of paper out of the desk drawer—"in an inside zipped pocket. As it seems to have to do with you, I was going to show it to you anyway. Not that it has any bearing on . . ." He let the words trail helplessly off.

Still holding the folded paper, he poured out the thoughts that had been gnawing at him. "If only I hadn't gotten lost— if I'd gotten home maybe twenty minutes sooner she might not have—and I was even going to stop and see you when I saw your car turn in at your place before ten, but I thought—"

Lydia cut in. "You couldn't have seen my car. I didn't take it out. I was dropped home, at one."

He gave her a dazed stare. "Maybe not," he said, as if it was pointless to try, now, to sort out the real from the unreal. Lydia, feeling very much the same way, took the little silver flask out of her handbag. Without taking time to think it over first, she said, "I found this on the car seat this morning. It's my father's."

"Then you might—I'm probably going crazy—read this. Well, you were going to anyway."

She forced herself to concentrate on the letter from Tom Hyde to her father, reading the words but not the sense of them.

"Turn it over," Darrell said. "Lally's writing, on the back."

*"Tell P. to tell L. one of the heirs died suddenly and he will now inherit that full share of the money."*

There was a long silence. Lydia's intelligence started to function in a frightened and unwilling way. "She went over there yesterday. Her glasses on the table in the studio . . ." Her voice dropped to a near-whisper. "I don't think he'd be strong enough to strangle her." She wondered if the brief darkness catching her meant she was going to faint. From it, she said, whispering still, "But in order to help you do I have to . . . ?"

From beyond the screen door, Mike Kaplan called crisply, "Police on the way in."

Darrell took the letter from her hand and pushed it into the pocket of her shirtdress. He stood up in a braced sort of way, then opened the door to Lieutenant Garcia.

He didn't know the social rules for such an occasion but he did know he wanted Lydia off the scene, and right away, for her own sake. "This is Lieutenant Garcia, Lydia," he said. "I'll see you later. Thanks for stopping by."

Garcia gave her a look which combined official scrutiny with male approval and made no attempt to interfere with her exit. He did, immediately, ask Darrell for her full name, address, and occupation, and how long he had known her. "Just in case we want to ask a question or two of your friends."

Then he got down to the inquiries he had brought along, first remarking, "That's an expensive watchdog you've got out there. Hyde Productions. He showed me his card. His shirt must have cost fifty dollars. Now then, we can't seem to find the filling station guy who gave you directions, anywhere within roughly a three-mile radius of Duff's house."

"Probably a night man," Darrell said. "But of course you'd already thought of that, and when you do find him on whatever shift he's on I'll be happy to go along with you for identification."

He felt bolstered, more in command of himself. Lydia's doing, of course.

"This business of your aunt screaming your name. When you were out. Why?"

"I suppose people in extreme terror—" Darrell began, and then for a moment couldn't go on, Lally seeing someone coming at her, death coming at her. He swallowed. "She might have thought I was on my way home, near home, even turning into the driveway. I have no other explanation."

Feeling that it was wiser at this point to answer questions and not ask them, he nevertheless bolted ahead. "*When* did she scream my name? *When* did she die? Will your medical evidence"—he couldn't bring himself to speak the word autopsy—"give you a clear idea of this?"

"Hot summer night, the closest any medical evidence can come is only approximate, it'll be give or take a certain amount of time, fifteen minutes, twenty, or more, at the very best." He glanced at his notebook. "Mrs. Martinez heard your name, the scream, about nine-twenty, or so she says, she seemed a bit vague about the exact time. Of course, we're talking to people along your route from Rio Grande to here to see if anyone saw a car—your car—stopped for a while, maybe you getting out, making a trip on foot to the house, and then coming back to your car to drive on to your sudden discovery." He delivered this information in a businesslike way. Was he hoping for a panicked look, or a twitch of pain and terror, as the finger unerringly found and touched the sore?

A fly landed on Darrell's neck below the ear. He brushed it off and the fly headed for Garcia's hairline, where it was again brushed off.

Garcia let a little silence stretch. He broke it, changing direction. "Did you know you were Mrs. Hyde's heir? The works?"

"Yes," Darrell said, and then in a verbal sidestep which could have been disastrous, "For the moment."

"What do you mean, for the moment?"

He could have bitten his tongue out. He saw the cliff he had already put one foot over. But it had sounded so black-and-white wrapped up, she dead and he the sole heir.

"She was worried about a niece in California who's having a hard time, divorced, two kids . . ."

"And you thought she might be going to include the niece in?"

"She didn't say anything about that. But she wanted to get ready to provide living quarters for her here, over the garage, if things got desperate."

"If things got desperate," Garcia repeated. His musical voice was neither friendly nor unfriendly, which made it harder to gauge him, deal with him. On the heels of this, he asked, "Where is your bank and how much money did you have in your account when you arrived here last Thursday?"

"I have no bank and no bank account. I live more or less by my—"

They both looked at his hands, long, strong, and brown.

Darrell saw that to anyone else the case being built against him was getting solider by the minute, brick cemented neatly to brick. He opened his mouth and closed it again. Keep Jerome, Jerome and the letter and the silver flask, until survival demanded producing Lydia's father as the man who might well have murdered Lally Hyde.

Lydia drove along Andalusia Trail in a not very purposeful way, her only purpose being to give herself time and space to try to think about several unthinkable things.

First and uppermost, would Darrell tell the policeman about her father? Would she, in his place? Probably soon, if not right away. The old, boiled-down, human end of the line: It's either me or you. Sorry.

But, as she slowed for a stop sign, she felt a crackling in the pocket of her dress. He had given it to her, Exhibit A.

Next unthinkable. A fantasy, a black one. Her father's Aunt Amelia must have left him a tidy sum after all, in a Swiss banking arrangement to spare him tax troubles. Seven years ago. Seven years of silence on his part. Lally must have found the carbon of the letter, and recently. She was not a woman to delay on matters which she felt to be of importance. She had come over to the house and told her old friend, Percival Jerome, to, briefly stated, cough up.

After about fifteen minutes of driving in the opposite direction from her house, she turned the car and went back. The police patrol car was still parked behind Mike Kaplan's Honda. Who, really, *was* Mike Kaplan?

What was Darrell saying to the police lieutenant now?

Leaving the Toyota at the side of the road near the adobe wall (why? because she thought she might have to run, escape from a great flailing black walking stick?), she went into the house and up the stairs. Her father's bedroom door stood a little open. She pushed it wide.

From his bed, his usually rosy face grayed against his down pillows, he demanded, "Where have you been? Why did you dash off and leave me all alone, all but immovably ill this morning, when you haven't any classes?"

"I found your flask in the car, on the front seat." Lydia placed it on the table beside him. Her voice was uninflected. "Where did you go last night in the car?"

She watched his jowls begin to quiver. She watched his facial bones seem to dissolve and the flesh turning into gray-purple jelly.

He gasped, "Lydia—"

"Here, wait a minute." She poured brandy from the decanter into his glass, and went and sat down in his armchair. "When you get your breath, go ahead."

It wasn't so much a matter of going ahead but of moving verbally backward, forward, and sideways, the blown gusts of words interrupted by a stifled sob here, a sucking pause for breath there. She sat quiet as iron and listened.

"I am guilty of a terrible deed, Lydia."

Her one interruption was right there, at the start.

"Strangling Lally Hyde?"

"No, no, no. I was going to talk it over with her, something she'd found in Tom's files that—the thing was, I couldn't bear to lose both of you, your mother and then you, and you would have been off like a shot . . . But when I got almost to her house, last night, I realized I'd been over-ambitious, my heart began to act up, the car felt as if it was going out of control, I knew I wasn't up to it."

He reached out a shaking hand and picked up his glass to finish the inch of brandy she had poured out for him. "But," (seeming to take it for granted that she knew all about whatever Lally had found in Tom's files) "while you were out this morning I called the San Francisco law firm. Funds will be transferred, funds to be deposited to your own bank account here, and then when I'm well enough we can make further arrangements and get the whole wretched business straight. Don't look at me like that. After all these years I can read your face, just as I always could tell what your mother was thinking . . . you're thinking this is a bribe. That I'm trying to bribe you with money, large sums of money. It would finally have been yours anyway, but as of up to now it's been mine, do you see that? Mine, to do with or not do with as I choose. But as for Lally, I did find the whole project beyond me and came home and put the car in the garage. Or, not straight home. When I turned from Andalusia onto Rio Grande I felt a dimming of the consciousness and drew off the road. Whether I fainted, or dozed, or convalesced in one way or another behind the wheel, I don't know. After a time I drove on, feeling that now I could make it, just about."

His shoulders and chest began to heave and tears poured down his face. Through the convulsion, he got out, "You do believe me, don't you, Lydia? That I had nothing, nothing whatever to do with—"

All that Lydia knew was that she couldn't bear this a moment longer. She got up from her chair and at the door she said, "Shall we leave it right there? Until we see what happens. About Darrell."

## 20

Mike Kaplan dealt with several dozen would-be gazers and even trespassers on the scene of the crime, cars slowing, some stopping. His formula was simple. "Property and road to be kept clear. Police orders." Several of those turned away said they were friends of Lally's. One elderly woman protested, "But I only came over to see if there was anything I could do —my God, poor Lally."

"Nephew's under sedation, not seeing anyone," Mike further explained to her. "Maybe tomorrow."

At one o'clock he knocked at the screen door. "Man here from the newspapers wants to know if you have a photo of your aunt."

"No," Darrell said, standing defensively in the hall shadows six feet from the door. He was sure that like most people Lally must have personal snapshots, but he was far from the point where he'd be able to go through, pry through, Lally's possessions, Lally's vanished present, and Lally's past.

"By the way, it's hot as hell out there, would you rather sit in the hall here? And what about food and drink?"

"Thanks, I'll stay in the car but I could use a beer if you have one. A sandwich if you're going to make one for yourself. Here's the paper. You're in it, in case you're interested."

Darrell in turn handed him out a cold can of beer, went back to the kitchen, and was startled to find himself hungry, but then he had had no breakfast. There was sliced ham in the refrigerator, and a wedge of paper-wrapped cheddar cheese. No bread, though. They were out of bread.

If he hadn't gotten lost Lally might have said this morning, "Will you pick me up a loaf of unsliced rye at the bakery?"

Toasted English muffins with mustard and butter would have to do for the sandwiches. He found for Kaplan's plate bottled gherkins and a ripe tomato to cut in quarters. When he went to the door his unofficial bodyguard was vigorously waving on its way a station-wagonload of people. Even from the back, he looked formidable. When the road was clear, Darrell called, and gave him his plate.

He ate his own sandwich at the kitchen table and then almost unwillingly opened the paper. But surely the police would have informed him first, accused and charged him first, if they'd found—found what?

The *Tribune* story was very much as it had appeared in the *Journal* this morning. There was an additional paragraph at the end, however. "This is the second strangling in several days of a woman alone in her house. On Tuesday, Mrs. Andrew Cove of 614 Mott Road was found strangled to death. Her husband, who was out of the state on a business trip at the time of her death, was contacted by the police Wednesday in Wichita, Kansas. Funeral arrangements are yet to be made."

The newspaper said it without saying it: was there a possible connection between the two stranglings?

Cove. Cove. Mrs. Andrew Cove. The name was in some way vaguely familiar, pressing an invisible button in his head. Why? He couldn't remember having read about her murder in the paper, he wasn't interested in local news and only, occasionally, scanned the nationally syndicated columnists.

Cove. In Lally's handwriting, sometime, somewhere . . . Mrs. Andrew Cove.

His hand went to his pocket for his wallet. He took out the scratch paper he had found by the phone, to take down the directions to Don Duff's house. There it was on the reverse side, penciled by Lally, Mrs. Andrew Cove, 614 Mott Road.

Without conscious thought or plan, he went out to the garage. He knew where Mott Road was because he'd picked up fresh fruit and vegetables for Lally in a small store there a few days back. He stopped at Mike Kaplan's car and said through the window, "I'm off on a small errand. Will you take over the house? I shouldn't be long."

He felt Kaplan's examining gaze, trying to assess whether he was drunk, or hysterical, or about to flee the scene. But there was a certain authority in his voice that made any of these themes unlikely. Anyway, Kaplan thought, I'm not about to follow him and maybe get myself strangled for my pains. Tony had given him no directives about following cars.

Darrell stopped the Pontiac at the chain link fence at number 614. He got out and gazed at the house set back from the road. There wasn't any information he could extract from Mrs. Cove, because Mrs. Cove was dead.

Why and when had Lally written down the name and address of a woman who a few days earlier had met the same death as she had? There must be a connection of some kind. Burrow for it.

From the right, where there was a white house stained with red dust standing close to the road, a man's voice said, "Looking for Mrs. Cove, are you?"

A man about his age emerged from behind a cedar tree, accompanied by a large unfriendly-looking German shepherd. The man held a can of beer and had a slight glaze in his muddy brown eyes which seemed to indicate that this wasn't by any means the first can. His hair was tawny and long, his sun-darkened face a mere collection of features which made no particular statement, except perhaps a slackness or shiftiness. He seemed to be secretly amused about something.

"I gather she's dead," Darrell said. "Do you live here?"

"No, place of my own, I come over now and then on my

afternoons off to give the old man a hand and the dog a run. I live where he don't get no exercise, too dangerous, right on Fourth Street. Name's Jones, they call me Junior here, my friends call me Eddie."

He seemed for some reason disposed to talk, maybe lonely after working away at giving his old man a hand. Darrell saw no point in hanging back. "Someone down the street from me was strangled last night. Same kind of thing, elderly woman, all alone."

"*She* wasn't elderly. Forty-five or so. But still mighty lively. When her husband was on the road, like he often is."

His lines were not very difficult to read between. Mighty lively meant men, probably entertained at her house, possibly including Eddie Jones, in whose eyes now appeared a flash of pleasurable reminiscence.

"I don't suppose you were here giving a hand on Tuesday?"

"Who wants to know and why?"

"I'm a private citizen," Darrell said, feeling the speed of his heartbeat picking up. "The woman up the street was kind to me, a good friend of mine."

"To cut it short—how much cash do you have on you?" They had been talking in normal tones over the chain link fence dividing the two properties, but with this question Jones's voice dropped.

"Depend's what's for sale."

"I was here. Every other week I work nights, this is my week for nights. I don't think anyone saw me. My pickup's on the blink and a friend dropped me off. I was mending a leak on the roof on the other side of"—he swiveled and pointed to the roof of the house—"that center chimney."

"But you couldn't see anything from the other side of the chimney."

"You could if you put your head around a bit and looked."

"You've told the police, I guess, about what you saw. If anything."

"Naw. I don't talk to police. They're no friends of mine."

Two cars going in opposite directions went by on Mott Road. Jones said, "Come on around to the back porch, it's cool there, the driveway gate's open."

On the porch, where they were hidden from passersby, and where for a minute or so Darrell felt a stirring of nervousness, Jones returned to the practical matter of finances. "How much did you say you'll spring for if I tell you all about it?"

He had his greenhouse money in his wallet. "Fifty dollars," he said, in a way that didn't suggest any bargaining.

"Okay. Let's see it first."

"In my hand, not yours, for the moment." He hesitated to get out his wallet and finger through the bills with this stranger's eyes watching. He might wind up with a clout on the head, no wallet and no information. "Do you think you could get me a beer?"

Jones opened the screen door and went into the kitchen. Darrell, with his back to the door, took out two twenties and a ten. The can of beer was handed to him cold and unopened.

Sitting down, Jones launched forth. "A man drove in, over there, about two-thirty. Old green Chevy, not his new Buick job. He put the car in the garage. I went back to my work, there wasn't much mystery about what he was doing there. After a while I heard music playing real loud, so I poked my head around the chimney again. His car was still in the garage, I'd have heard him leave. In a minute or so a beat-up black Volks drove in, and an old woman got out of the car and went to the front door and then around the side of the house, I guess to look in a window. The music was still playing. Hey, friend, open your beer, you're sweating bullets. She was back there at the side a minute or so, I had to laugh, what she was probably getting a load of, in the bedroom, then she left fast. There was a big white dog on the front seat of the car. Still the music, crazy. Then maybe three, four minutes after she left, he did too, must've gone into the garage from inside the house. I saw the doors open up and the Chevy going down the drive and out. That's it, until I saw the papers next day. And she had no other visitors that afternoon."

Hardly able to breathe, Darrell asked, "You know who the man was? You said, not his new Buick job, so—"

Jones absentmindedly patted the head of the dog lying panting beside his chair. "Yeah, I know who he is. Jack Rolt, owns the Double-Ace used-car place on North Fourth. Sonofabitch sold me a used Dodge pickup a few years back, hoked up to run okay for three weeks or so, then whammo, junk on wheels was about the size of it. I tried to get my money back or some kind of satisfaction and he dug in and said I must have mishandled the old wreck. Anyway, I've seen him here before, on and off for two or three months, when Cove's away."

Appearing much flattered by the rapt attention he was getting, he went on, "Course, it's anybody's guess, but you can have mine thrown in for free. She was crazy about him, that I know. He's married to a blond bag of a wife with lots of money, show-off home, swimming pool, in the Northeast Heights, the works. Say she says to him, Mrs. Cove, that she can't live without him and all that garbage, that they'll both get divorced and coo together forever, says she'll let his wife know all about the setup otherwise. I can sort of see it, or hear it. Then, whammo."

Was it malice, revenge, that was making Jones so forthcoming? He had said the police were no friends of his (Darrell when he heard that had envisioned a jail sentence or so) and here was a way to plunge the knife in the back.

And, as he proceeded to make clear immediately, without the chance of placing himself in any possible future danger.

When the fifty dollars changed hands, he said, "Now that I've got it, and you've got the picture, get this. I never saw a thing, I didn't tell you anything, I wasn't here that afternoon, and if you say I told you all this I'll say you're a liar and that I never laid eyes on you before. Fair's fair, you got what you came for, but if you ever try to connect it with me you're down the drain, fella. I'm nobody's witness now or ever. I guess you understand what I'm saying?"

Darrell finally opened his beer, which had been held tightly in his clamped hand, and took a long deep swallow. "I seem to get your drift," he said. "Okay. Thanks." He set the half-finished can on the scarred round table and walked away to the Pontiac.

Driving home, he thought fleetingly of going to the police, to Garcia, and handing the whole thing over to them.

In answer, his mind formulated a short script.

Who told you all this?

Someone who happened to be passing by while . . . I didn't get his name.

What'd he do, just stop his car when he saw you at the Coves' gate and decide to pour it all out to you? Or maybe you said you might be a suspect in another strangling and could he help out?

If he took another approach with the police, and gave Eddie Jones's name, and said he was watching the scene from behind a chimney next door, Jones would no doubt follow his own script.

If he had any kind of prison record, his testimony would be of questionable value.

And if he turned the whole thing around, as he very well could when approached by authority—

The guy, Hyde, gave me fifty dollars to tell you what he told me to tell you.

Forget, for the moment, the police.

It was only when he was putting the car in the garage that the rest of it hit him. An elderly woman in a Volkswagen. A white dog.

He had had the Pontiac on Tuesday. The Martinezes had a

black Volkswagen. The dog was probably Parma. None of this made any immediate sense to him. Except that it seemed quite clear that it had been Lally, going around the side of the house and maybe seeing something she shouldn't have seen. And that wasn't necessarily limited to an afternoon romp in bed.

Mike Kaplan had to be gotten rid of before anything could be made to happen. At five-thirty, Darrell went out to his car and said, "Look, everything's under control. You've done a great job. Thanks. I'm going to have something to eat and take the phone off the hook, I've had it for today."

Tony Hyde's orders to Kaplan had been: "Stay for the day, two jobs. Take care of nosies and nuisances. And if he seems to be coming to any kind of boil, call Geraldine." Geraldine was, among other things, Tony's personal secretary as against his office staff of secretaries. "You couldn't be expected to deal with that kind of thing anyway, we'd have to get the big boys in. Geraldine's all briefed and ready."

Darrell, Kaplan thought, looked calm enough, in fact amazingly calm, something about his face, a carved appearance. But sober, and from the pupils of his eyes and the way he walked and the steadiness of his gestures not on anything.

"Okay." With a glance at his watch, "I can catch the next flight or so to L.A. Good luck. Take care." He drove off with a wave.

Darrell went into the house and consulted the directory for several telephone numbers. The yellow pages offered the number of Double-Ace Quality Used Cars, and the white pages the home number of Rolt, J. There was only one Rolt in the book.

Try the office first. A sloppy-voiced young male answered. "The boss is busy out on the lot, fat chance I can drag him to the phone when he's shoving a sale—"

"Tell him," Darrell interrupted, "that it's important. Tell him that it's a matter of life and death."

"Okay, okay, he'll still say no, but I'll tell him. He hasn't got much of a sense of humor when he's busy."

There was a wait of about forty seconds and then another voice said, "Yes, who is it?" Tight short syllables but maybe that was the way Jack Rolt always talked.

"My name is Darrell Hyde." His voice was tight too, the words hard to get out, and they must get out firm and clear, totally understandable. "I've found a little item among my aunt's things that I have to talk to you about privately. Mrs. Thomas Hyde, you know. The woman who was strangled last night. I'm not at home right now but I will be at home around eight-thirty. I suppose you know the address?"

"No." He thought he felt shock along the line.

"Andalusia Trail, number 437—not too far east of Mott Road. See you, I hope." Don't embroider, don't explain. Darrell hung up.

Let him have it naked.

21

"Don's at a party," his secretary said, adding chattily, "if you'd call it a party, opening of a new Atlas Copy Center office, a lot of small-time business types, attendance by station brass obligatory. He was groaning before he left. Want the number?"

"Yes." Duff would probably not want any part of his own invitation, or, rather, desperate request, but the only thing he could do was to try.

The telephone was answered and somebody said he'd go and look for Don Duff. There was a lot of background noise, rock music, laughter, a wave of voices.

"Who?" asked Duff, coming on the line. "Louder, please."

Darrell said who, and said loudly, "Something important— can you hear me?"

"Not in this happy hellhole. Wait, I'll go out into the lobby and call you from a pay phone, give me your number again."

When, a minute and a half later, he called back, Darrell plunged in headlong. "I have a hell of a favor to ask you. There's someone who might be coming here to the house around eight-thirty who may know a lot about who killed my aunt. But he may think I may know a lot about him and I don't want to—I mean—" He finished simply, "He might not even turn up. If he does, nothing may happen but something might. I'm all alone here."

After the briefest hesitation—natural enough, Duff hardly knew him—Duff said, "All right. Tell you what. I'll go home first and bring along my tape recorder, and then if there's a ruckus you can give us the rights to the tape." Then, more warmly, spontaneously, "Hang on, friend, I'm all but at your side. Give me the timing as you see it."

"I told him eight-thirty because it starts getting dusk then, but he might want to take me by surprise and come a little earlier. If you could get here, say, about seven forty-five?"

"No problem."

"Don't stop your car in front of the house. There's a place for sale across the street and for all I know he might be watching from there. There's a narrow road off Andalusia, Santa Lucia, going toward the mountains, two houses west of this one. Turn your car down that road and cross the fields behind the houses until you come to the third house, adobe. Come in through the gardens in the back. They're walled and connecting. I'll go and take the padlock off the outer door. That way, you'll be completely hidden from anyone across the street. Got it?"

"In spades," Duff said.

"I promise there's no danger for you. You can go into my aunt's bedroom, close the door, lock it. You're an ear. I need an ear. Just in case."

"See you, Sherlock—with the ear all tuned up."

It was close to six, the sunlight brilliantly slanting, the great-tailed grackles imperiously claiming the very tops of the trees for their jubilant evening music.

Darrell looked around him, considering. First he locked up the house. Yes—pull the shades down—didn't people in houses of mourning do that?

You didn't have to enter a house to invade it with a bullet.

A bullet . . . he went to the closet in Tom's office, took down the Browning, reached for the box of ammunition, and loaded it. He carried the shotgun into the living room and propped it where it could not be seen against the back of the wing chair. From a kitchen drawer he took two of Lally's old but highly efficient carbon steel knifes, a long one and a medium-length one, honed them against her carborundum stick, and put them at the front in the desk drawer near Lally's chair. After a moment's thought, he took out the medium-length knife and placed it behind the long lacquered black-and-gold Chinese box, which held odds and ends, on the top of the chest in the hall.

Would Rolt, if he came at all, come to the front door? The juniper formed a thorough shield, concealing any approaching visitor from the Martinez house. But don't bank on it, give a thought to the back door. He found Lally's heavy wooden meat mallet and laid it on the windowsill near the door between the pulled-down shade and the flowered café curtain. He'd see to the padlock on the outer garden door about seven-thirty.

His nerves jumped as the phone rang. Rose Martinez, in a voice which had a small-girl scared tone, said, "I was just finishing up the supper dishes and putting away what's left of the chili, and I thought . . . do you have anything to eat over there? I could warm it up for you. I wouldn't want to upset your privacy, I could just leave it for you, hot, on the doorstep."

Like food put down for the dog, Darrell thought. But kind, even though it was clear that she didn't want to come into a house that held him.

"I've got everything I want, thanks very much anyway." Everything I want, a gun, knives, a meat mallet. And a stomachful of tension and fear.

What if Duff was, right now, getting drunk at the Atlas Copy Center party and seeing things from a different point of view? Saying, Oh, to hell with it.

He walked from room to room, not so much to check security, such as it was, but because he was unable to sit down, to eat or read or have a beer. In the kitchen, a light wind moved the drawn shade a little. He hadn't wanted to pull the windows down. Too hot, too claustrophobic, the closed-in feeling would be, and sounds outside, any sound of anyone approaching, would be blanked out.

If he did close the windows and started up the air conditioner in the living-room window there would be a humming cover-up of outside noises.

The screens were all latched from the inside. Not much of a barrier but an awkward and attention-signaling way of plunging into a house, you might be caught with one leg over the sill before you could get your knife or your gun out or ready your hands for the throat.

What would he do in the other man's shoes? Come earlier than expected, or later than expected? Or not come at all? Suspecting a police trap, just stay away? But, after that phone call, "Andalusia Trail . . . not too far east of Mott Road," could he afford to hang back, even for a little while, a day or so? Still trying to find his way around in the other man's mind, Darrell thought that he'd think, If the police had any kind of evidence, they'd come straight to me, not screw around with a rendezvous at the house of a dead woman.

Don Duff turned off Andalusia down Santa Lucia, drove three blocks east, and parked his car off the road in front of an empty sagging warehouse, some obscure failed place of business, the faded words "Hay, Feed, and Grain" painted above the door.

He was no outdoorsman and as he crossed the long field carrying his tape recorder he was afraid of putting his foot into some unexpected hole and spraining an ankle. Or startling up a waiting rattlesnake. But the snakes were mostly in rocky places, in the mountains, weren't they? This field seemed mighty damned near the mountains. Maybe the rattlers liked to spend their early summers among meadow grasses and wildflowers.

He assessed himself as being about 85 percent sober, which was pretty good after being affable to one and all at the Atlas party and especially considering the adventure he had allowed himself to be invited into.

He saw with relief the honey-colored walls of the enclosed gardens, to his far left. He turned as he passed two old twisted apple trees and headed for the outer gate, which as promised was not padlocked.

Turning to close the door behind him and wondering if there was an inside bolt somewhere high or low he should shoot, he saw himself against the green, and the flowers, and the shadowed walls, in the long oval mirror inside the door. He also saw, almost too fast to be registered on the astonished brain, a dark rising swift movement close behind him, a man's face, before a fist was raised and he was struck a frightful blow behind the ear. But the pain vanished along with his consciousness.

Darrell heard with almost unbelieving relief the light knock on the kitchen door. The clock over the table said seven forty-five, on the nose. He opened the door to a stranger.

A man three inches or so over his height, toughly built, dark glasses, duck-billed cap, work clothes. The man stepped confidently into the kitchen. "Ryan, from Chávez Tree Service," he said. "Were you the folks that called?"

"No," Darrell said, in a freeze of fear. He leaned to his left and felt under the edge of the shade for the meat mallet. The man reached to his right and lifted the shade, picked up the mallet from the sill, and put it back again.

"Look," he said. "I've got the wrong house but maybe in a way it's the right house. Maybe I can be of some help to you. I happened to be driving by here at around nine o'clock last night and I saw a Toyota pull into the drive. This old guy with a heavy stick got out and began hobbling toward the front door. He looked sneaky to me. No business of mine, but when I read about the murder in the papers, I didn't see anything about *him*. Now, thinking back, it might be someone you know." With an air of doing his civic duty, he added, "People see things and sometimes keep them to themselves. It's not right."

Darrell was torn. Where was Duff? Had he gotten drunk after all? Had this man, random in style as his information was, really seen Percival Jerome approaching the house? How could he make up a Percival Jerome, walking with a heavy stick? How could he guess Jerome had any reason for visiting Lally? And the right car, the Toyota—

The man could be telling the truth or twisting the truth; but he saw no way of dismissing, denying, the car, Jerome, the walking stick.

On the other hand—

The mallet was no longer much good to him. If he made a dive for it the man could grab his wrist. He wanted badly to be in the near proximity of the shotgun and the knives. Just in case.

The telephone came briefly to his aid. Hardly knowing what he was doing, he went toward the living room, where his protection lay, to answer it.

Had he heard behind him the small sound of the kitchen bolt sliding home?

The man followed him into the living room in what seemed to be an indecisive way. Darrell faced him as he picked up the phone. He could hardly be attacked during this operation, he could say to whoever it was, "There's a man here, right here, who may or may not be thinking of killing me."

An out-of-control unfamiliar voice, either a baritone female or tenor male, started in immediately, "Murderer! Monster! You'll never get away with this, you—" After the fourth obscenity in a row, Darrell hung up.

"You're sure that you don't want any tree work done while

I'm here to take the order?" the man just inside the doorway asked.

Other subjects dropped, Jerome dropped, death of an aunt dropped. Except, would it be with him forever, even if the police couldn't find enough evidence to arrest him?

Or, framing the words he was about to speak, was he—just the merest disappearing flash of a thought—laying his life on the line, all but asking for death himself, because he hadn't been there to prevent Lally's?

Go ahead, say it. If the man was who he said he was, no real harm could come of it.

He moved over to the side of the wing chair. "No, no tree work, and I don't want a used car either. Your name is Jack Rolt." Now, a quick necessary lie: "I saw you in your own car lot, I drove past it today after I finally heard what happened to Mrs. Cove on Mott Road."

How long did the silence last, five seconds, ten? "Rolt?" The raise of the man's eyebrows was visible over the tops of his dark glasses. "That's news to me." His face began to shape itself differently, but Darrell thought, Well, every face in a nightmare looks distorted, out of kilter.

"My aunt was over there that afternoon and saw what was going on. It must have taken you a couple of days to find out who she was and where she lived, and then you walked in here and strangled her."

The man, now only six feet away, the length of his own height, made a lightning dive at him and pinned him against the wall. His hands were on Darrell's neck, arms braced wide at shoulder level shielding his head from Darrell's fists. Darrell kicked, kneed, got out a half shout, half scream, but the man was a heavy muffling force holding him to the wall, perhaps thirty pounds heavier than he was. The iron thumbs, the agonizing thumbs. Kick, fight, try to . . . oh God, oh Christ . . .

There was, dim to his ears, a sudden ripping sound at the

side window and something hit the floor with a crash. A confusion of movement, a sense on his part rather than a sight of someone hurling himself through the window, a sense of a raised hand with an object in it, a thump and a roar of pain, not his pain, and the grip on his throat loosened. A sense of pressure gone and a body hitting the floor. Then a merciful dark haze, was this death?

He opened his eyes half a minute later to the feeling of a hand on his chest, holding him up. Duff's face, looming close, blurring over, close again.

"You're okay," he said. "Here, sit down. I'll find you a drink if there's anything in the house. But first things first."

Darrell collapsed into the wing chair. He managed to bend his head a little forward to look down. As he did, vomit rose in his throat and spilled on a shoulder on the floor near his feet. Jack Rolt lay sprawled there, eyes closed, blood pouring from under his duck-billed cap down one side of his face.

He heard Duff talking to—yes, it must be the police. "I may have killed the bastard while he was doing his best to kill someone else, maybe you'd better bring an ambulance along too. Yes—of course—I'll tie him up anyway."

He yanked down one of the sill-length sprigged dimity curtains at the window with the burst-out screen. Darrell whispered, "Desk drawer," and Duff went to it and took out the kitchen knife. He jabbed it into the center of the curtain, tore the fabric into two lengths, and bent down. Turning Rolt ungently over onto his face, he tied his wrists behind him with one curtain length and bound his ankles with the other.

He stood up and heaved a long sigh. "Two scores paid off. He knocked me cold in the garden, he must have been waiting there, listening, I suppose, getting his bearings. Then when I came to, the bloody back door was locked, but I heard you all but giving your last hurrah and—" He waved at the screenless window. "Where's the necessary?"

"Kitchen cabinet . . ."

Duff came back with a bottle of scotch and two glasses. Another wave of nausea hit Darrell at the first gulp but he forced it back. "God almighty, the green man in person," Duff said, watching him anxiously. "Drink it down. If you throw it up, there's more in the bottle."

Who was it who was still panting, gasping? Not Duff.

"Here, give me your arm, we'll put you on the sofa. It shouldn't be long before they . . ."

Four minutes later the police arrived.

Jerome, after the several days of cowering in his bedroom, in his bed, showed himself able, just about, to make it to the dining room for his breakfast. In a frail voice, he asked Lydia for a soft-boiled egg and a piece of thinly buttered toast. "And tea instead of coffee, I think."

"Here's your paper while I cook," Lydia said, offering it without further comment.

From the kitchen she heard thirty seconds later his explosive "Good God!"

She brought in his breakfast and sat down at the table with her own cup of coffee. He said, "And to think that man might have been there in the house, or coming toward it, when I—"

"Yes, that's one point to consider," Lydia said. "And there's also the fact that Darrell just got off by the skin of his teeth, or of someone named Don Duff's teeth. I thought that that was a rather appalling part of the story too. As well as your fortunate deliverance from whatever you were going to do." She took a sip of her coffee. "What exactly was it again? And how close to the house did you actually get?"

"I turned around perhaps ten feet from the door. In my confusion and distress—and giddiness—I walked into the clump of iris. And I told you, don't make me repeat my humiliations, I was just going to . . . plead with her, face to face, to let me manage my own affairs in my own way in my own time. Now that ample funds will be becoming available, I'll have lost you anyway, I suppose."

Lydia found, angrily, that she was sorry for him. He would provide his own punishment, loss of pride (perhaps temporary considering his nature) and loneliness, even though physically speaking she wouldn't be far away. Unless Darrell had other plans.

"If there's money enough, I'd suggest you take a long sea journey, say the *QE2*," she said. "That will give us both time to put ourselves back together again and it ought to be, the salt air and rest and everything, terribly good for you."

A knock on the frame of the screen door, a voice, Jennifer's, calling, "Anyone home? Darrell?"

It was eleven o'clock on the sunny Monday morning. He went, for the time being well past finding anything startling, to the door and let her in.

She looked alien here, she looked New York, Upper East Side. Bone-colored loose linen coat, long voluminous linen skirt, tortoise-buttoned on one side, leopard-patterned silk shirt, mahogany shine of hair, delicate float of perfume about her. And chatter, fast easy chatter, at the ready.

"I am so sorry, I meant to make the cremation service but we were hung up over Dallas forever. You can take the will for the deed. Poor Lally. Was the service ghastly? But so much better than a bells-on funeral." She explained away what might have looked like family feeling by saying, "We were on our way to La Jolla, the three of us, to shoot commercials, so I thought, Why not stop off, kneel down and all that, and then catch an afternoon plane to San Diego? Would you be shocked if I asked for a drink? I'm off my Perrier water for a bit. And do join me, you look a little awful, but then why shouldn't you?"

As he went from the living room toward the kitchen she called after him, "You even made the New York *Times.* Dad-

P03

dy's name, I suppose, and Tony and all that but still—*I've never made the Times except the advertising column now and then."*

As they sat down with their drinks, she said, "And what are your plans? You're not going to stay here in this . . . outback?" He thought that the chatter was not as heartlessly superficial as it sounded; she was trying to pull a shielding veil of words over his brush with death, Lally's terrible end, ugly dark unlikely things that tended to dim momentarily one's enjoyment of life.

"Yes, I'm going to stay here for a while anyway. I have the house and the property. Some money along with it, more, as a matter of fact, than I expected. I have a job I'm going to start this week. I have two jobs, really." He looked at his hands, which had busied themselves for an hour yesterday with clay that was springing to life.

"And I have . . ."

"As long as it's what you want," Jennifer interrupted, studying the yellow pages in the directory, head bent. "I must call a cab and dash to the airport. I hate leaving you alone like this—"

Lydia had just appeared, as if in affirmation of his last three syllables, in the doorway after coming in from the back gardens. Her eyes were still remembering tears but her armful of flowers held scent, and color, and hope.

Darrell got up and went over to her and said to his sister, "But I won't be alone."

## About the Author

Mary McMullen, who comes from a family of mystery writers, was awarded the Mystery Writers of America's Best First Mystery Award for her book *Strangle Hold*. Her other books include *A Grave Without Flowers, Until Death Do Us Part,* and *Better Off Dead.*